As You Desire

As You Desire

by
Madeline Moore

spinsters ink
minneapolis, mn

Copyright © 1993 by Madeline Moore
All rights reserved.

First edition.
10-9-8-7-6-5-3-2-1

Spinsters Ink
P.O. Box 300170
Minneapolis, MN 55403

Cover art, "Om Mani Padme Hum (Oh My Body Pains Me So)" by Max L. White

Production by: Sacha Bush   Lori Loughney
                Melanie Cockrell   LouAnn Matossian
                Ellen Hawley   Mev Miller
                Kelly Kager   Liz Tufte

This is a work of fiction. Any similarity to persons living or dead is a coincidence.

Printed in the U.S.A. on acid-free paper.

As You Desire by Madeline Moore
Library of Congress Catalog Card Number: 93-84275
ISBN: 0-933216-95-5: $9.95

As You Desire

Dedication

To the memory of my beloved brother,
George Moore, Jr.
and
My mother, Clara N. Moore,
whose emotional and financial generosity helped
make this novel possible.

Acknowledgements
❖❖❖

I want to thank my writing consultant, Dorothy Wall, for her brilliant advice and dedication to my work.

I'm also indebted to my tireless and loyal typist, Zoë Sodja.

Spinsters editor Ellen Hawley made editorial suggestions which were immensely helpful to me.

The support of my friends in San Francisco who write—especially Janell Moon and Mary Wings—has been indispensable to me.

Finally, I appreciate the encouragement given me by my students and colleagues at the University of California, Santa Cruz.

Every character in

As You Desire

is purely fictional.

Any similarities to persons living or dead

is coincidental.

Part One

Prologue

Journey

1

I had already lost her when the anxiety attacks began. I said, "I am hyperventilating again, Cecilia."

"Breathe, and feel your feet resting solidly on the floor," she says.

I throw myself at her feet and move slowly up her legs. My head is almost on her inner thigh when she begins to pull my face up her stomach, all the while smoothing the sweat from my burning forehead. I notice the delicate square fingers and the turquoise ring lighting up her left hand. And I see that her life line is longer than mine.

Cecilia always walks away from me in the Berkeley Art Center, and in other places as well. She wears white cotton shirts unbuttoned low over her breasts most of the time.

My father told me once that he went swimming with Bonnie and Clyde and that he dated Bonnie. I believed him. I believe my father and I were lovers in a former life, and I believe that in another life my daughter Jessica and I were twins. I am reunited with her only briefly in order to be her mother. I believe that in a former life Cecilia and I were Greek athletes locked in the daily struggle of opposition. We took up the battle only four years ago, and my mind became sick. I lay on my bed, frightened and stifled by my own icy breathing, and my friend chanted for me, chanting on the flattened floor. During that long night my body levitated and Cecilia mounted her enormous black steed and severed my bleeding chest.

"If we stay together we'll destroy each other, like the Taurus and Capricorn we are," she said. I thought, What a betrayer she is!

I kept reaching for my friend's hand and saying, "Shouldn't we go to the hospital tonight? I am flying away." But she said, "No, we'll make it to the morning." I had never before tasted the iron and the water commingling on my tongue. My saliva tasted of iron for many months.

I once had a cousin in a hospital having a nervous breakdown. She would throw her arms around my neck like this. I wanted to kill her, but I couldn't because she wanted to kill herself.

Yet the morning did break and my friend got up and ran out to call other friends, leaving me for hours as she searched for the telephone. She said, "The karma from your former life is breaking out of you now." Then an enormous chameleon popped out of my left breast, and my Shakespeare teacher gave me a shot in my brain. I believe it was all a dream. But I'm not certain.

Cecilia always says, "You don't have to edit with me."

Then I become encouraged. So I jump right in.

I say, "Cecilia, I love you."

She says, "No, you idealize me."

I say, "Okay, I idealize you."

She says, "You idealize me so you can idealize yourself."

I say, "No, I'm really attracted to you."

She says, "You just use sex to distance our friendship."

The next morning the moon shone red. Blood hid the whole waking world, where the Virginia creepers crawled down the boarded place of my birth and I was four again. I was abandoned in a hotel room. Yes, abandoned! My mother said, "We won't let you breathe in that noxious dust. We must protect you from your asthma." The hotel door remained locked all night. The policeman hid behind my closet, silently blowing soap bubbles at me. He never moved at all.

Soon it was time to move, and the movers were there. Despite the fact that my father and brother beg me to join them in heaven, I reply, "You will not see one jot of my body until I tell my story." Oh yes, the time may even come when my little children, after a long day's labor, return to me. Annie, my daughter, will once again paint her purple and green watercolors. Annie, who once said, "God is an artist walking over the Paris rooftops, painting them pink and yellow." And Cynthia, my other daughter, will wear her pink ballet shoes, her severe black hair swinging like a lion's mane over the stages of her ambition, her long torso trembling with love.

And Jessica—I am coming to Jessica.

The next day came, and the movers were coming, and an iron rod seemed to jam itself up the back of my spine, all the way to my skull. Someone once said that the conditions of one's birth are repeated in myriads of patterns. So perhaps my erupting cycles of despair and desire are not unlike the seventeen hours it took my mother to push me toward a new beginning, only to let me fall back into the darkness, and then, finally, into the light.

Cecilia, when will we drink wine from the Loire Valley and bicycle into the gleaming golden chateaus? The violins are hovering over the head of the beloved singing, "Dare we begin again, my lover?" Mendelssohn sits down to compose his *Concerto No. 1 in E minor.*

So the next day the movers came, and somehow I got up and dressed in a black dress and asked Jessica what we would do. She—child that she is—stood like an Amazon queen, were the histories rewritten. My beautiful daughter told the rough men about my grandmother's bed, bolted and rebolted from numberless moves. The truckbed was open. I laughed at the sight of all those antiques flapping in the sheeted wind.

Then my friends, one by one, walked through the big door because it was morning. They came and I said, "Do you love me?" and they said, "Yes, Elizabeth, we do love you."

2

"Votre billet, s'il vous plaît, Madame."

He's so officious and squat. But is he a policeman? I like the sound of his syllables.

"Squat" is a sexual word, isn't it? Is he really a ticket collector or a policeman? I can't tell.

"Your ticket, Madame," I translate.

If the conductor really wants it, I'll give him my ticket. But have I exchanged enough money? I can't remember. I see the sign for trains going from Marseilles to Aix. I've left San Francisco, left Paris. I'm going to Aix, there is no doubt about that. My phrasebook is red—yes, now I've spotted it. I so despise this black backpack. I'm much too old for it. I only carry it for the sake of my students.

Even at night, a feverish wet heat rises in the Paris streets. I thought, better to travel at night than risk these anxiety attacks—with the untimely heat wave and the crowds. At the Gare de Lyon, I ran from porter to porter, saying, "Where is the train for Marseilles?" But they told me nothing. Somehow I found it, with all its Frenchmen and plastic seats. So this is the last leg of my trip—twenty-seven hours....

Marseilles is like a French oven, and my blue denim jacket clings to my back. I clutch the black gate to steady myself. The train for Aix is just on the other side. The French voices surrounding me sound like the chants of Holy Rollers I heard so long ago—those Cajun voices rising out of the streets of Lafayette, Louisiana. I was an anemic child. I hated the chipped white paint on their dirty wooden churches.

Now the Frenchmen are shoving me, fighting for their seats. Mine is already reserved. I keep repeating that fact. I've memorized the seat number: *trente-sept*. No one can have it but me.

"Cézanne's atelier is in Aix! Don't you dare miss it, young lady." An old woman across the aisle speaks to me in French. I feel too numb to respond. I think to myself, "Look out the train window—don't break your concentration."

"You are a writer."—Repeat it. "I am a writer."

I have made a house exchange with a French lawyer from Fuveau, and there, surely, I'll write my first novel. I've always succeeded in work ... and Cecilia will love me when the novel is published.

"I am a novelist—the novel works through me—I am a medium—I am a me—"

The woman laughs and looks down at her water bottle. I watch her, look down at my book, *Antigone*, my model of courage, which always brings me good luck.

Certainly I have the knack still. "Weeping willows in back gardens." I'll write *that* for Cecilia. "We are passing the village of Gardannne. The corn grows too close."

The passengers sleep with their cigarettes teetering on the edge of their lips. There is no cold water to be found. I dare not sleep. I must try to stop the convulsive tic in my left eye. I must try to still the myriad images battering down this train.

Perhaps Cecilia will write me at Fuveau. I'll dedicate the novel to her. I think of her. I imagine the call has finally come. I think of the last scene. "Will you meet me for tea, Elizabeth?" We are both in the village of St. Ives in Cornwall for the summer. "Yes, I'll be right there." I run through the sloping streets of the village. The grey granite buildings gleam with the morning sun. Pink bougainvillea bloom in miniature gardens. The tea shop is adjacent to an emerald-green door, and she sits near the window, smiling at me, her red tie loose and her white cotton shirt open at the neck.

"I want to stay with you forever," I say. "I want to feel the solidity of your arms and the coolness of your cheeks on mine."

I look down at my watch. 4:30 p.m. A wave of nausea rises through my body and lodges in my throat. My throat is so tight, slammed shut like an oyster shell. I haven't eaten for hours...feel like the iron rod is jammed up my back, trying to break out through my skull.

"Look, the windows are made of stained glass in those little farm houses." A beautiful man next to me speaks French slowly, with little or no accent. Perhaps he's an artist from Paris looking for the light Cézanne captured on his canvases so long ago.

Still, it's impossible to believe that I'm sitting in a

five-car train, cutting through the countryside in the middle of the afternoon. People around me look like French country actors. But I love the colors outside. Cezanne didn't exaggerate the orange soil when he painted his landscapes. I think of it as stacked squares of children's clay. And all the houses are white with red roofs. I can imagine the French countrywomen inside them making breakfasts of heavy cream and hot French bread in the early mornings. Mt. Sainte-Victoire is there in the distance: nothing, really, but arid limestone. Yet I see the pink glow over it, as if it were softly sad because of its aridity.

"I see you're a reader. Why *Antigone?*" he says to me. For the smallest space of a moment I remember there *was* a past life—there *was* a purpose different from this endless present, this travel toward some unattainable, undefinable recovery.

"I'm a professor," I reply quietly. *"Antigone's* a woman my students can admire. I sometimes wish I had her defiance."

"Don't you?" he asks.

He's the only person who's kind, the only one since I've been away, and I wish I *were* brave and strong. But I've lost even the smallest fantasy of myself as defiant. The boy I imagined myself to be—yes, that tragic boy that all my female students worshipped. Perhaps I'll never find him again. It was Virginia Woolf who said, "He who takes away our illusions takes away our life." My students loved that quote.

I look up and the man is smiling at me! With his white tennis shoes and grey *blouson* shirt open at the neck, he's seductive, like Cecilia. Can it be possible that she's come back to apologize to me?

"Why didn't you let me hold you?" I reprimand her.

"Why didn't you stay and talk it through with me?"

The man touches me gently on the arm. He speaks quietly in English now. "You're on a train headed for Aix," he says. "You've confused me for someone else."

He will just have to realize I'm a professor! It's not an unpardonable sin, this confusion.

"You could be Cecilia's twin. My vacillation is perfectly understandable," I speak to him in my imagination.

"Tell me about your students," he interrupts again. "Do you miss them?"

I hate the pity in his voice. I jerk my dark glasses out of the backpack and cover my eyes... just ignore his patronizing question. I wish I could go home now, not to Berkeley with its health food lesbians and the Hari Krishnas, but home to Lafayette—to the South—to the race to which I belong. But I am shivering, yes, shaking uncontrollably, knowing that their beliefs are no longer my own. I have only one home, with Jessica. Wherever she may be.

I remember our last day together, her perfectly arched eyebrows and baby-thin honey hair still curling at the nape of her neck. I remember the rush, the white bicycle helmet and the leather fingerless gloves.

"I won't wear them, Mother."

"You will if you care about your life, sweetheart."

I wished then that my daughter would cry, just once when we parted. I waited for her rage, for her to call me weak and hypocritical. I waited for her accusations. I knew she hated my decision. She would move now to Santa Monica in her senior year of high school. She would have to live with her father in a small bachelor apartment. "How could one's mother, one's protector, love a woman so stupidly that she would throw aside her own family?" But Jessica refused to say Cecilia's name. And I had no other alternatives. I thought then of Jessica's fifth birthday and her training- wheel bike. How she rode like a pro down our bumpy Berkeley driveway while her older sisters and I formed a safety net out in the street. Five years later, we rented bikes in Napa Valley, sauntering through the vineyards, laughing in the leaves. At least Cynthia, dancing in Manhattan, has made it, and Annie is safe studying art history at N.Y.U.

"If you won't talk about your students, at least tell me about your family," he insists. "You seem dazed."

"They no longer need me," I say. "I don't want to talk about them, either."

"What will you do in Aix?" he asks.

"I'm going on to Fuveau."

"Someone will meet you?"

"No."

"You'll need a taxi. There's no public transportation. Are American friends going to join you later?" he asks.

"No," I reply.

When the train stops, he leads me to a waiting taxi. He begs the driver to communicate with me in simple French phrases. I am afraid of the cab driver. He refuses to look me in the eye, and he keeps laughing to himself as if remembering a successful tête-à-tête from the evening before.

I notice the cab is unmetered. I accuse him of this purposeful omission. He laughs again. Has he unzipped his trousers or does it just look that way? He winks at me in his rear-view mirror. I feel afraid that he will drive into a back alley and rape me. "Stop the cab," I demand. But he drives on in a leisurely manner, parodying the informative and impersonal tones of a tour guide whose English is only half learned. "Don't miss the scenes, miss," he jokes. "We pass but once, I think." "The highway between Aix and Fuveau is quaint, the littlest in zee world," he laughs. "See the village of Palette—like a painter's easel."

The stark white granite of Mont Sainte Victoire is an awakening of sorts from this nightmare. This black night of an afternoon. My driver continues to drive even more slowly. "Pont de Beaeux is the dullest town in the world," he says.

"When will we reach Fuveau?" I ask.

"Only two more miles, your highness," he jibes. "Just relax! Aix and Fuveau are only five miles apart."

We drive through Le Canel and Le Barque, before I see a tiny sign which reads "Fuveau."

"The address, Mademoiselle?" he asks.

"*Trois, rue de Fivoli.* Yes. *Trois,*" I reply.

We drive to the square in the southern part of the little village of Fuveau. I can smell the dust, and the shadows of the silver poplar trees loom inordinately large along the lanes of the village outskirts. Except for those poplar trees, I have the distinct impression of being in another town: the Mexican town of Tijuana. My ex-husband, Paul, and I stop there on our long journey to Mexico City. Is it the summer of 1963? In a black van decorated with red poppies, an irate man waits impatiently for a young woman. Then, as now, it's 5:30 in the afternoon, that crazy hiatus between day and night when people drink to numb their loneliness. The waiting man sees a little figure in blue turn the corner; he quickly motions to two other men in his van. They place a large piece of cotton over the woman's nose and mouth. Then, as if she is a newly cleaned carpet en route to its owner, they pitch her through the back doors of the van. When I tell Paul about the incident, he says, "It's horrible, but we mustn't interfere with a foreigner's marital problems."

This evening in Fuveau, I am besieged by sighing sounds. Are the women inside its wrought-iron gates also being smothered by cotton covered with ether? Are their husbands fat and hairy, or are they dashing French intellectuals driven to violence by the violence of their jealous sensibilities? I dare not look at my driver.

The dark comes on suddenly, and the acrid taste of rusty iron permeates my mouth. I am so hungry that my vision blurs. Is my driver a terrorist? Is he a radical Communist who mistakenly imagines me to be an American conservative? How terrible my life has become. He pockets a black revolver as he puts on his brakes, bringing the cab to a violent stop. Who in Fuveau can save me from him?

"If we stay together we'll destroy each other, like the Taurus and Capricorn we are," Cecilia said. And I am so sad!

Isn't it paradoxical that we can show one another our passion only by renouncing our future together? What a dishonest way out of our complicated affair, I think.

"Here is the address, Mademoiselle," he says. He stands up ceremoniously, bowing slightly at the waist: his trousers are definitely zipped. With the two large leather cases under my arms, I give the driver thirty francs. I've overpaid him, but I no longer care. I step forward, open the rusty black gate, and see a long line of poplars leading to the house. The driveway has the appearance of an unkempt English country lane and it seems to go on forever. Where is the house? I must try to calm myself. The place is strangely unlit. I should have ordered the cab driver to flash on his headlights. Is the entry through the back garden? Yes, that must account for the delay.

The cab's muffler pops, so finally my driver has left me alone.

And then I see them! Where the house should be, granite headstones dot the enormous graveyard. Some of the tombs are raised like the ancient fortresses I have seen on the Sussex Downs in Southern England. The streets keep struggling up a pinheaded hill, but the cedar trees swirl like angry dancing women tearing up the ground that protects their sleeping husbands.

I set down my luggage and walk back to the street. The address has to be wrong, but there it is again—"3"—on the wrought-iron gates. I stagger back; my feet feel like pieces of ice. When I walk into the graveyard for a last look, I see, out of the corner of my eye, an old man placing a large white lily on someone's black grave. For a moment I want to run to him and say, "Save me, old man, and I'll comfort you." But I dare not trust anyone.

Words like "cockatrice" and "homeless" come from my own mouth. I begin to cry. Where is the center of town? I walk along a darkened lane filled with gravel. Frogs are croaking in the ditch. Is the thin woman with her anorexic girl-child who seems to be pointing toward a light really standing in the center of the lane? There's a building! But l'Hôtel Joyeux is locked, as if a senile owner has forgotten his evening guests—even though it can't be later than 6 p.m. I see lights in a tavern, and to my relief there's an open door and a sign: Le Club Joyeux. Both the same. From the doors I hear singing. Is that Edith Piaf's voice beckoning me to come in and warm myself?

There, at least, someone will feed me.

When I walk in, two French farmers are hand-wrestling. Near the bar, six dirty men in overalls make bets on the winner.

The room is swaying, and the smoke is so thick I can't breathe. Get to the window, I think. Go as far as the bar. Ask for a sandwich.

"Je voudrais un sandwich au jambon."

But I can no longer see. My throat is fiery, then dry ice.

I kneel. Pretend to pick up a dropped coin. Place palms flat on the floor. Can't faint here. Can't lose myself here. Strange insect noises. Everything like dirty dishwater. Ears are clogged with it. High buzzing noises. Can't make out the French words. Like millions of bristling crickets. Hear only "*triste*," "*triste*,"—"sad," they're saying. And then the waves of black vapors seal me off.

When I open my eyes, I don't know where I am. My mind sees two eyes—yellow fox eyes, unrelenting eyes. And the walls hold no pictures. I think Paris, Paris—some cheap hotel in Paris.

3

His eyes are steely blue, with such intensity! Like the eyes of someone in my family. Perhaps my Irish grandfather with his little alcoholic stomach, yes, like my poor grandfather's stomach. He offers me a cup of cold water and lifts me to a caned chair.

"I'm hypoglycemic. I waited too long to eat."

Calvin Hersey Douglas is old, and he speaks English. He assures me he's an internist practicing in Paris. "Let me take you to a hotel. They'll book you for the night. I'm on vacation from Paris, staying in Fuveau with a friend."

The frayed hole in his grey cashmere sweater is incongruous somehow, and why the fresh black dirt at the bottom of his khaki trousers? "I'll take care of you if you'll allow me. There will be no other doctor for miles."

I try to reason with myself. I wonder if I can stand up and walk.

"Is your hypoglycemia serious?" he persists.

"Yes, it's complicated by other things. By the asthma..."

"I think I see."

He brings me an orange and a large piece of brie.

"Try them, my dear."

When I swallow the brie, it lodges in my throat like the suffocation the dead tolerate. I reach for the water. He holds my head to the edge, and I swallow in great gulps.

Very little choice. Talking to no one and everyone really.

"Please do find me a room tonight. Tomorrow I'll be okay."

Curious French eyes glitter as we walk past the hotel desk. His skinny arms hold me up. He lifts an enormous rusted lock and places me on a bed as if I'm an old rag doll. The room is small and brown.

"I will leave you only long enough to find the concièrge. You'll need your own key to your room. I'll keep this spare one."

After he leaves I stare at an undersized chest of drawers with brown woolen socks stacked on top. Whoever was here before me, he forgot his socks! The bed is cheap and feels more like a cot than a bed. Next to the chest, a shabby Directoire table supports two photographs of twin girls—ten years old, probably—dressed in matching white blouses. How incongruous it all is. Perhaps these girls are the owner's daughters.

As Calvin Douglas comes back into the room, he hands me a card:

>Calvin Douglas, M.D.
>Specialiste à l' endocrinologie
>Institut Pasteur
>Paris

"You see my prestigious credentials? What you can't know about is my breakthrough in diabetes."

But I don't want to hear any more.

"I have brought the key to your room." Tears in his eyes, the curious sympathy of this stranger. "In the morning, we'll see Fuveau in a new and brighter light. Don't worry, my friend's house is nearby. I'm not far from you."

I want only to sink into the grey surfaces of sleep. He has left me staring at a mirror in the middle of this shabby room. The woman in the mirror is so pale; her dark circles dominate the face. I've never seen my pupils so small...like the pupils of lost marsupials. The bed is filthy and hot. The bedspread, once white chenille, is hardly more than a rag. I wish I had asked that doctor to leave some cheese and crackers. Outside the window, a tree branch hits the pane. Cecilia said that women are acculturated to confuse fear with excitement. Did I fear her? I felt faint in her room that day. Everything in her room was vivid: shiny white cotton chairs, a bluebird flying past the window. She waited there for me imperiously playful in a tall red chair.

"How are you feeling?"

"I'm terribly frightened, Cecilia. I've made a house exchange with a French lawyer from Fuveau. I'll be away for the year, hopefully working on a novel."

"You're frightened about the trip."

"I'm frightened because I'm losing you. I can't sustain a trip in my condition without you."

"Are you willing to try an experiment?"

"Hell, you know I'll try it."

"Close your eyes, then. Imagine I'll buy you anything and it'll be with you always to remind you of me. What do you choose?"

"A red enamel rocking horse in the center of a toy store, lit up with ruby lights."

"I've bought him for you. Now what?"

"The red rocking horse and I crash through the toy store window and out into the sky. We are the size of giants as we fly through the air. I have a feeling of weightlessness and well-being."

"Where do you fly, Elizabeth?"

"We soar over the Atlantic...so high that the water sparkles silver below. As we reach southern England, we slowly descend...then there's a backfire like exhaust from a jet. I sing as I ride over the Sussex Downs scarred brown with the lines of Roman roads. Can we see each other at the end of the year, Cecilia?"

"No, we should separate. I'll call you in Fuveau later—just to touch base."

4

When I awake the next morning, my white shirt is soaking from sweat. I can't remember where I am. There's a knock at the door; I reach down for my watch, hear my own voice speaking, my own heart beating!

"Who is it? What do you want?"

"It's Dr. Douglas. I am your endocrinologist. Don't you remember?"

"Yes, yes, I'm coming." I pull up my rumpled trousers, open the door.

"You collapsed last night in the bar. Remember?"

"I do remember. But where are we today?"

"Don't be afraid. You're still in l'Hôtel Joyeux. I've brought you a soft-boiled egg with French toast and orange juice. People who are hypoglycemic need small amounts of protein at close intervals."

I need to establish a time sequence. Yesterday was Paris, today Fuveau. Looking around I see the sunlight hitting the window. Outside, the bright day looks oblivious to my illness. I'm aware of my clothes thrown in a heap on the floor, as if I were frantically trying to find my nightgown late in the night.

I avoid the doctor's eyes, get back into bed, and pull up the covers. He looks embarrassed as he hands me the breakfast.

"Why are you here in Fuveau?" He finally breaks the silence.

The impulse to cry is overwhelming. Make up a story... that's my job, isn't it?

"First let me drink my juice. Shall I call you Dr. Douglas?"

"We are both Americans! Can't we dispense with such formalities?"

"I admit I should have stopped in Aix."

"Ah yes, Aix—an excellent city—a gourmand's delight— "

"No, Aix is a place to study French, there at the University. Master a new language and live in the present. That was my hope."

"There's much to forget. Yes, I know there *is* much to forget. May I call you Elizabeth?"

"Yes, why not?" He's just a sad, sad person.

"But why Fuveau, Elizabeth?"

"I'm writing my first novel, you see, and a man, an artist friend of mine from San Francisco, described the town graveyard here. The slant of the landscape is perfect. And the tombstones are glorious. They go back to the fifteenth century. I hear that Napoleon's father is buried here. I need that graveyard for my opening scene."

Dr. Calvin Douglas pales now and he avoids my gaze.

"I came straight here to see it! That's all! I didn't measure my strength."

"Elizabeth, by all means, there's only one graveyard here! We'll see it today."

I steal a look at him. He smiles reassuringly.

"You're an American?"

"Yes, Boston. Same Douglas as Supreme Court Justice Douglas. Our great-grandfather came to Boston in 1850."

"Do you have children?"

"One daughter, Renée. She was both a daughter and a son to me, a child of my middle age."

"Does she live here in Fuveau?"

"She's far away. You look a little like her around the eyes. Are you a swimmer?"

"I ride horses—or I once did." I see him staring at my nose.

"When Renée was fifteen, we took a thirty-mile bicycle trip through the Loire Valley. The coach said she needed to push the limits of her strength." Suddenly he looks very angry. I see him pull out a silver flask from his coat pocket and then put it back.

"If you'll wait for me downstairs, I'll dress—and we can walk through Fuveau, Dr. Douglas."

He gets up abruptly.

In the dusty, shimmering light, the orange roofs glow deeply red. Surely my house will appear today. Maybe next to the graveyard: last night it was just too dark. As we walk through the labyrinthine lanes, there's a low, free-standing rock wall, defining the side of a Provençal garden.

"Wasn't that wall built by the Romans?"

"Yes. The Romans occupied Marseilles in 120 B.C.

They built quickly on a large scale because they were specialists with building equipment. Their earliest walls were made of local limestone."

"Walls are so odd, aren't they?"

"Their original walls, like these, were merely dry stones held in place by their own weight. Later they added iron clamps, and by the first century A.D., they filled in the cavities with a cement constructed from mortared rubble."

He's such a pedant. I wonder if he supports the student uprising in Paris.

"Why are *you* here?"

He hesitates. "Each summer," he measures each word, "I return to place flowers on my wife's grave. We are, I guess, drawn to the same graveyard—for different reasons."

Who is this man? So appealing and yet so strange.

As if reading my mind, he replies, "In my prime, Fuveau was the site of my summer practice. My wife and I loved the heat and the mountains and the simplicity of village life."

"And do you love them now?"

"Yes, but I'm alone now. No one sees them with me. I'm like an aging cat whose body is still lithe but whose spirit is dead. Go out in the alley, old black cat, we no longer love you."

"I'll stand with you today. We'll both honor your wife's memory."

As we walk along the greying, dusty lanes of Fuveau, I see a small grove of olive trees, all silvery green like my first prom dress. So many years, and what have I to show?—stop that, stop it, Elizabeth!—and then there again staring at me, running amok amongst the olive trees, the anorexic woman and her solitary starving daughter. I will not listen to them—just my fatigue—I'll switch to French.

"*Je suis très fatiguée, Dr. Calvin.*"

"*Oui, mademoiselle. Nous nous reposons.*"

Calvin carefully holds my hand. "Let's eat an early lunch. I need the rest as much as you do."

"I have to stop here before we walk." I want to call him Calvin now. I want to believe he's like an older brother who had an untimely tragedy but has recovered his life, his career.

"Just look at the flowers for a while, Elizabeth. So often they are all we have."

All around I recognize the pungent aroma of lavender and sage...see the broad translucent leaves of a sage plant growing out of the limestone, which peels in patches from the grey-brown soil. These leaves are like delicate broad wings of blue dragonflies. I begin to feel at home in my body after I find them.

"Calvin, I've lost someone I love."

"Yes, we've both had losses. Sometimes you lose someone even though they're not dead. We'll be good for each other."

Calvin takes me to a tiny sidewalk café. The tables are covered with red linen. Our lunch consists of *bouillabaisse, vin rouge* and *salade composée*. I feel giddy as we eat, as though I might speak a little French to the waiter, who insists on *crème caramel* for dessert.

The afternoon is slow and dreamy. When Dr. Douglas places irises on his wife's grave, I pretend a kind of objective interest.

"This graveyard will have to be photographed. It's perfect for my novel. I want to examine these epitaphs, these useless truisms people say to one another when someone dies."

"Is there someone I should call? I mean about your hypoglycemia and your nervousness?"

Looking down at a black gravestone, I think of my mother's indifference. Certain sentences rush through my mind.

"Why don't you find me a new son-in-law, Elizabeth, to straighten out my finances?"

"You will not obliterate my lesbianism, Mother."

Despite my anger, I remember feeling lonely when she doesn't call. And when I complain, she replies, "Honey, I can't call you when I'm depressed. It's not fair to you." So I usually call, expecting the long list of complaints, the slur of sadness in her voice.

Mothers' Day is worst.

"I've wasted my life, Elizabeth," she always begins. "I see families with their sons, and I think of your brother's suicide, and I know I'm a complete failure."

"I miss him, too, Mother."

"Yes, but it's never like a mother's grief."

Shortly after my brother's suicide, my mother turned to me one day and said, "If we hadn't spent so much money on you, this might never have come about."

Calvin clears his throat. "Is there someone I should call?" he repeats.

"No," I reply.

Part Two

Descent

5

At 5 a.m. we begin our train journey back to Marseilles, and then on to Paris. Calvin lives in Paris where he practices medicine out of his house—"In my old age," he says. I notice an angry, furtive look in his eyes. He's offered to put me up, to strengthen and calm me, he says. I've got to find out what happened to my house in Fuveau. I won't stay in Paris long, though I don't know yet where else to go. As Marseilles draws nearer, I see mulberry trees and oleander bushes hugging the highways. Morning lorries are plying their trade. One hauls an enormous trailer of red and white Ford Fiestas toward a red crane. I think of Stephen Crane's *The Red Badge of Courage*. Even now, I long for my students.

The harbor at Marseilles is smaller than I remember. Ugly black ships deface its zircon waters. Along the shores, one can see modern apartments constructed of granite and grey limestone, along with colorful billboards advertising "Umberti Wines" and *"Engins Griffet."*

Here in the station, the waiting room feels like an oven, like a nineteenth-century English prison with people sleeping feet-to-face on the floor. Its walls are grey concrete buttressed with wrought iron, too small for the many who sleep there. Men from India and hippies from California lie sprawled on their backpacks and filthy bedding. An old French grandmother and her grandson sit huddled against a wall. They are oblivious to the radios and the announcements of arrivals and departures to Arles, Avignon, and Aix.

At the gate, three English hippies with frizzy hair and black net stockings clatter in their spiked heels down the rampway to the fast train bound for Paris. Several gaunt Turkish men shove their way into a line of latecomers clamoring for the *couchettes* which may still be available.

Boarding the streamlined train, I shiver in the false cool of the air conditioning. The tray at my knees comes down like the trays in a plane's interior. Grotesque, this orange-walled cleanliness and the saucer of Mediterranean outside the window, with tiny white boats veering and colliding. On the top of a granite mountain, two oaks are intertwined as if holding each other from falling off the precipice. As the train climbs, the tracks below them hover over the ground like disappearing lines of mercury.

On the outskirts of Arles, the landscape is yellow with sunflowers and constantly shifting light. Small silver poplars dance in the foreground and black cedars whirl behind them. Thousands of them. Van Gogh asked to be imprisoned in a mental hospital in Arles. Why? And incessantly, there are Calvin's words—"I," "me," "mine"—in a tunnel of echoes. The pristine sounds of a tour guide. At the Gare de Lyon,

Calvin takes me to his silver Citroën, and drives us through the throbbing streets.

As we approach what Calvin has called home, the Parisian streets widen. Fashionable young women with slim black jackets walk in and out of outdoor cafes. A man in a scanty red shirt stands strumming a guitar outside le Café Select.

"Look at what's happening on the rue Départ. Just plain Americanized," Calvin complains. "Bowling alleys and horrendous parking lots everywhere." In the direction of the avenue du Maine, I see a large crane swing over a building. Why is it swinging?

"At the turn of the century, avant-garde artists and poets moved from the Left Bank to our neighborhood, to Montparnasse," he says. "A place called the Beehive at No. 52 rue de Dantzig became the studios for Modigliani, Chagall and Léger. Talk went on for hours in the cafés along the boulevard de Montparnasse. You know, I was not always the famous doctor I became. As a young man in Boston, I painted landscapes. Now I am proud to live among artists again, the only doctor on the street."

As the Citroën nears the house, I hear jackhammers jamming into black asphalt, feel them stabbing at my temples. "Used cars being flattened for reuse. Two streets from our own." Calvin clips his angry words. The Citroën stops abruptly, and there in the front, two monsters flank a wide entry to a massive door. They have the wings of eagles, the bodies of lions. But their heads—what are they?

"Those two are my gruff griffins," he jokes. "This will become your home away from home."

We walk, then, into an old house which stands tall on the rue Froidevaux adjacent to the Cimetière

Montparnasse. Two large floor-to-ceiling windows in front emphasize the clarity of its seventeenth-century architecture.

"Courage." He leads me by the arm.

"Here, Elizabeth, here on my shiny Queen Anne chest. So all the world knows—here's a picture of Renée and her mother!"

The thirteen-year-old does indeed look like me. Dressed in navy-blue seersucker cotton shorts and a heavily starched white blouse, she holds a wooden tennis racket in her right hand. But she's thin—too thin, I think. Next to her is a woman in a white linen suit with long auburn hair and green eyes which seem to say, "See, my daughter has known all the benefits of tennis. Next she'll go on to dance."

"Renée was quite a tomboy in those days," Calvin says. He hurries me into a gigantic living room covered with multitudes of rugs.

"Where is she now?"

At first he doesn't respond. Then he enunciates each syllable.

"She is disinherited. She is a lesbian."

Glancing down at the red and yellow carpet beneath me, I'm surprised to see the circular dizzying patterns staring up at me.

"Get me something, Calvin."

"Would you care for some tea, or perhaps some Pernod?"

"Tea—that's all—thanks."

"Sit here," he advises. Looking around, I see only a high, bench-like piece of furniture whose mahogany legs are carved with rabbits and minotaurs rushing into the dark rich wood.

When he returns with the tea, I move to a chair

whose back is woven with some rush or cane material, with legs shaped in half circles.

"That's American oak," Calvin says, "an antique from the 19th century. Sit there. This was all to have belonged to Renée some day. And then she made a foolish decision."

The golden tea warms my chest. I want to rise up, get up....

"What's Pernod, Calvin? I don't know about it."

"Pernod smells like licorice candy and is the color of mother's milk. Have some!"

"I don't want it. I told you tea was just fine. I'm curious about Renée's mother, though." My voice is too loud, as if the volume weren't my own.

"Her mother loved Sonia Delaunay's clothing and Van Gogh's passionate colors."

"Yes, I'm intrigued with Van Gogh's brilliance and his insanity," I reply. "Did Renée's mother study his insanity?"

"Her mother was a collector, not a dabbler in the perverse."

Abruptly Calvin leads me to his study and places a print of Van Gogh's *Starry Night* in my hands.

"This house will become your friend, you'll see."

Down a long dark hall, he opens the door to what he calls his guest bedroom. Outlandish blue satin chairs match the coverlet on an enormous mahogany bed. There is no fresh air.

"Just sleep in your slip," he says. "Tomorrow we'll unpack."

I won't sleep in my slip, I think. It makes me feel like an orphan.

That night I stare at Van Gogh's *Starry Night* and the glaring yellow stars above my blue window sash.

My mind tries to discern some far-off scale, some copybook of shining geometrical shapes. The lion lies down with the bear...the swan floats slowly through the coral purple clouds.

Where are the constellations? I can locate myself in the constellations!

Did Renée's mother watch the constellations outside this old house pushed up against a cemetery? I wish she were my mother, too. What strange names are carved into the dead stones? Just now are they hurling themselves through the rectangular leaded windows up at the front of the house? I get up to lock the door and fall back into a burning sleep.

The man who calls himself my doctor never leaves me alone. Why is he still there in the late hours of the night? I count his footsteps as he paces between my room and the high, leaded windows. Is he waiting for the mother's ghost to re-enter him? Will she re-enter me? I walk quietly to the door, kneel, and look through the keyhole. He stops outside my door. His breathing is strained and loud. Does he whisper my name? "Elizabeth, Elizabeth, are you there for me, my darling?" I hurry to bed. I am two years old again, trying to sleep in a tiny bed with a vaporizer blowing warm air toward me. I finally stop coughing and slide down, still nauseated, into an uneasy unconsciousness. An enormous black spider crawls slowly up my vaporizer. When it reaches the top, its face is half spider and half man. And then it melts into a black slime.

"Elizabeth, Elizabeth!"

"Is that you, Mother? He still waits outside my door, Mother, even now."

I bind myself to the soft contours of the bed and stare at a crumpled railroad ticket—enunciating the foreign syllables, the French which was meant to help me live in the present.

❖❖❖

There is a stillness to the next morning and the white lilies open gently to the sun. I open the heavy leaded window and the perfume of the blue irises awakens me to the scent of dark roasted coffee being brewed nearby. Were it not for this time and this place, this space of no place, I could imagine myself a bride breathing the warm air of a Parisian morning. A young Italian woman shyly stands at the bedroom door. "I am Mia, your doctor's summer chef. He eats peanut-butter-and-jelly sandwiches all winter, but in the summer he entertains, and I do the cooking. He's already begun work in his study, but your breakfast is served."

Mia covers my thin body with one of her own terry-cloth robes.

"Hurry up, the coffee won't wait," Mia says.

A nickel-silver basket of various sugary biscuits and French bread sits in the middle of a stark white linen tablecloth. Mia carries two thick white pitchers to the table and pours the dark, hot coffee from the first. From the second, she fills up my blue mug with frothy milk. "Calvin says that you must have mostly chèvre and French bread," Mia admonishes. "Never too much sugar."

I nod and smile at Mia as if I'd always lived with such limitations. She passes me red raspberries lodged in a delicate silvery china dish adorned with miniature blue birds. I'm so hungry my hands tremble as I slab the French bread with heavy pieces of cheese.

Something in me remembers a constant hollowness, so I barely restrain my tears of relief.

"Does Calvin forbid sugar in my coffee?" I am half-serious in my compliance with her.

"Just be moderate."

I observe the floral leaded scrolls in the doors of the china cabinet and a silver butter dish within, shaped like a Chinese pagoda. I will remember to ask Calvin what his wife's name is and where she was born. I drink half the coffee in one gulp. I will remember to ask Calvin about the mother—Renée's mother, not mine. Suddenly Calvin appears.

"Elizabeth, my dear, you've met Mia. She cooks for me in the summers—the season to entertain, you know. She'll give you the perfect delicacies for your hypoglycemia!"

My skin feels hot. I feel faint. I hear his voice again—our driving through Paris, was it only yesterday?—"The City of Love," he said in a hushed voice—the motors humming like nightmares—"The Notre Dame," he said in a louder voice—and tiny people hurrying like leprechauns into that church, which looked like a stage set to me. Still looking, still waiting for Cecilia to deliver me, my lover to speak to me.

6

Four days pass, one much like the other. I get up, dress, plan to look for my own apartment, but then I realize I don't know how to begin. And then the dizziness sets in—the hot yellow splitting headaches, the searing years of wandering after my brother, the spinning years. "You can't keep saving him," some voice intervenes, but I see him in the stars. "I need something," I say, but no one answers. Only Calvin's words come back: "You need balance. Your own blood betrays you." Yet he knows nothing of betrayal. Of Cecilia's betrayal. Cecilia *is* my own blood, Calvin, and no one here even knows her name. And then I try again. I get up, dress, prepare to go my way, but there's no place to go. I must find new names, new doctors, I think. The telephone book's all in French.

How can I speak their language, Cecilia, when I've forgotten our own? How we talked that last.... Did you say "I don't want to..."? Or did you whisper, "I can't let you—anymore—," Cecilia? Were you crying? Tell me again why we had to separate. I want your arms around me.

As if drawn on by some magnet, I walk toward Calvin's study. I'm troubled by doubts I'd never voice. I need to see Calvin's degrees framed. Some wall will hold them. And perhaps his study is a dark and quiet place where I can bring Cecilia back.

But the room is small, a doctor's study. In the corner, a black, cracked leather recliner sags with age and determination. Calvin's book shelves are mostly empty! I run my fingers over the spines, medical texts with titles like *Endocrinology: A Logical Approach for Clinicians* and *Diabetes in Adolescents.* Propped next to his book on diabetes is *Alice in Wonderland.* Odd. I laugh but shrink at the sound of my voice. And the walls are strangely vacant. No framed degrees here.

Crossing to the window on the other side of Calvin's library, I turn, walk downstairs to a smaller study, and sit down at a small round table. An old cardboard box hides in the corner of the room. A lavender folder rests exactly in the center—as if a very old teacher were trying once again to encourage her pupil to write her morning composition. Will it shred? Suddenly it's become important to me. "Go on, open it," I say to myself. And there atop the title page in small spiky letters I read:

> Renée Douglas for her friend Germaine—
> Desire. It is that and that alone which we
> end up caring about.

And then—nothing! Perhaps I'll finish it for Renée. Perhaps that's all we do: complete one another's longings. But what would I say? That my devouring physical hunger for Cecilia was never reciprocated? That I am pale with weariness and wandering and now wonder if I can drown myself in the rivers of my desire? That in fleeing from her body, I stamped its power into my soul? That Cecilia has delivered me to Calvin—has left me? I pick up a pen. Maybe my writing will call out to Renée. Maybe she's living nearby in Paris, wanting to come home again, never imagining that her American sister has arrived. I'll begin.

Once, a long, long time ago, there were two strong beautiful women who lived together on the ancient coast of California.

But Mia appears. "Doctor sent me with some tea. Doesn't want you neglected and all moody again."

I crumple my paper. It's no good, anyway. Sentimental rot, I think. I must get out, start looking for a flat. It's been four mornings since I've seen the sun. I go to the bedroom. How should I dress? Is the Paris spring still hot? Simple and clean, I think, my white cotton trousers and a green shirt. Like the pleasant grass growing, clean and happy. After all, you're travelling....

Calvin's marble door is as heavy as a giant bank vault. I strain against it. The sun's cold purple eye startles me when I step into the street, as if I had forgotten the pain of light. I've read this story somewhere before, about a girl struggling for the sun, reaching for her....

The people walking are tiny wind-up dolls, talking a fast gibberish I can't understand. And the smoking—terrible, like the entire world is swimming in a cold grey haze. They walk right into you on the sidewalks and blow their smoke into your eyes. I stop for a café au lait. I think I've read—in some guidebook maybe—about how early the Parisian cafés open, about the fact that Parisians revel in people's differences whereas Americans...

"Un café, s'il vous plaît!"

"Bien, madame," he replies.

As the waiter writes my ticket, he moves from table to table. He is very handsome but unshaven. He looks as if he's writing a violent opera and composing it in his mind despite the café's rubble and the selfish diners. At the next table a man turns his hand over and back, over and back examining his thumbnail. For some reason I think of Eliot's line about corpses and gardens. Does it go, "that corpse you planted last year in your garden"? His lines always strike me as ironic: "You who were with me in the ships at Mylae/ that corpse you planted last year in your garden/ Has it begun to sprout?"

Odd how the only language I really hear is from books—*The Waste Land*—things which call out for explanation—imprint their messages and then disappear....

Here's a franc. Place it under the salt shaker. Get out! I walk more quickly along the boulevard Edgar Quinet. Follow the signs to the cemetery: I can begin my research at least. The Cimetiére Montparnasse stretches over the hill. On the other side is Calvin's house.

I cross the street and wander through a graveyard like an enormous park, with rows and rows of raised headstones. Men with wheelbarrows and precision clippers tiptoe quietly in and out of the dirt paths. So much silence. Everything moves slowly, as if in a movie. The men clip the grass in rows. The birds chirp, but I can't hear their voices. I need to hear the sound of my own voice. The gatekeeper. I'll try to speak to him. He looks like a decent man.

"I'm a researcher from America. I'm looking for Baudelaire's cenotaph."

"South section—number 14—along the rue Èmile Rickard," he says.

"South section?" I take out my map. Yes, it's there, near the avenue du Midi. The resting place of the famous.

I don't let go for a minute. I may lose my direction.

"Why not?" my other voice comes in. "You're no longer pursued by madness. Enjoy Paris. Live a little!"

"It's still there," I think. "That other voice."

I relax my jaw a little bit.

"Let yourself go," the voice continues. "Remember your dreams!"

"Okay, okay."

I smile. No one's there to see me smile. I can smile as much as I want to now.

I sit down and pull out my map. Looks like I'm on the avenue de l'Est. My heart's up in my throat, a useless heart. I feel like scolding it. "I'm too far from home," I say to my heart.

"Look around," the good voice coaches. "You're safe here."

And then I remember it. Last night I dreamed it.

I'm arguing with my mother. My oldest daughter looks on disapprovingly. We live in a wooden shack and I slam a rickety screen door. I run away from my mother. Maybe it's Louisiana, maybe Florida. My father and I walk through the basement of an enormous city parking lot. Its grey concrete walls keep spiralling into the ground. We go deeper and deeper. We keep searching and searching. "We haven't lost our car," he assures me. "We've just forgotten the right floor," I agree. We run down one more level and find the same slot, number 4, only now it's in a blue section, next to a concrete pillar. "That's where it was yesterday." I assure him. But we're still on the wrong level. So we run down one more level, and still it's not there. We run back up. "This is the place"—I'm insistent now—"where we parked the car. But every time we return it's missing."

"Do you think it's been stolen?" he asks me.

"Yes. Stolen, or I forgot to secure the hand brake." He begins to cry.

"My insurance policy is fine, father. Please don't cry." I touch his cold cheek. Unfolding the crisply folded policy, I'm aware that one sentence hides in miniature type at the left-hand corner of the page.

"Liability for stolen or totalled automobiles—$20."

But that's not enough!! For this life of sorrow, for my Irish peasant father returned from the dead, with dirt clinging to his wet woolen trousers inching out of the ground, eyes blazing with hatred and hard work.

"Get up, Elizabeth!" my good voice says. "Look around you!"

❖❖❖

And then I hear them. An American couple. Country people, maybe. She smooths her skirt.

"Did you ever see anything like this, John? This black marble headstone with a Valentine heart and a picture?"

"The man's not been dead long, and there's already notes to him."

"I believe he's a famous rock singer," the woman ventures, turning to me. "Got any ideas?"

Her accent comforts me, thrills me almost.

"No more than you do," I reply. "But we can imagine he was some ladykiller."

She blushes.

"What's *your* name?" she asks.

"Elizabeth," I smile. No one's *really* wanted to know my name since I left Berkeley.

"And what's yours? Are you from the South?" I'm pleased with my assertiveness.

"Mary Sue," she replies. "How do you do."

The rhythmic sound of her words smooths the sharp edges of my anger and loneliness. Something in me begins to open again. She reminds me of my first friend, little Jane, dressed in pink organdy, with her tiny fingers.

"We're from Gatlinburg, Tennessee," she answers. Looking down at her feet, I think her high heels must hurt her toes.

"Yeah." He smooths his beige polyester suit coat. "Mary Sue and I love Tennessee. We're in agricultural management."

"We raise corn and tend chickens, just like his daddy did. What do you do?" she asks.

"I do research." I try to keep calm.

"Research?" he asks. "You do it in a cemetery?"

"Baudelaire's here; rather, his cenotaph's here!"

"Cenotaph? What's that?" He looks uneasily at his wife.

"I'm sorry. It's a statue. I'm looking for his head on top of a statue and his body beneath—you know, and his body underneath the ground."

They both laugh.

"You're okay," he says.

"You look kind of pale to me." Mary Sue moves closer.

"It's just all this research. This...writing. I'm doing an analysis of Baudelaire's poetry."

"Why work when Paris is so fun?" she asks. "Why work in Paris?"

"I work because I'm waiting for—" I stop. "I write because I'm under contract to the best publisher...."

"You getting enough iron?" Mary Sue touches my shoulder.

A car is symbolic of identity, we lost our—

"You getting enough iron?" she persists. "You living with good people?"

"Yes, yes, the best of people! With a very old doctor and his wife. She cooks, but he's senile, I'm afraid. I'm in the way. You two know where to look for apartments in Paris?"

He steps back, but I persist.

"What about the others on the trip? Does your tour guide have friends in Paris?"

"Why?" she asks.

"I need to be on my own. I *may* be anemic, and I can't ask *them* for favors. My French is so bad, you see. I should never have come."

They look at me in disbelief.

"Why don't you go back to America?" the man asks.

"Because I don't have the strength just yet." I see them stiffen. "Will you ask your tour guide about accommodations?"

"We're pretty limited by the tour. We have to stay on schedule. Why don't you give us your phone number? We'll ask him and call from our hotel."

He hands me a pencil and an old laundry ticket.

"Here!" I reply. "Don't forget, please."

I see him pocket the ticket and slowly guide his wife out of the cemetery.

"We'll call! We sure will, little lady." But I know they won't.

As I walk past his ancient grave, Baudelaire's carved laconic lips seem to twitch in recognition. Quickly I cross the street to the surprised laughter of French children on an outing with their teacher.

> *Au clair de la lune*
> *Mon ami Pierrot*
> *Prête-moi ta plume*
> *Pour écrire un mot.*
> *Ma chandelle est morte*
> *Je n'ai plus de feu*
> *Prête-moi ta plume*
> *Pour l'amour de Dieu.*

Did I ever sing such a song?

7

It's 6 a.m. Some birds are shrieking at the top of their lungs outside my window. I'm trying to awaken from my dreams—blue bizarre bedrooms. My younger brother still calls me, wants to gather me to him, and I have to keep testing. What is mortality? What is immortality? I've never written about it. I thought I would. And I didn't visit his grave because I didn't believe he was dead. Not for twenty years, I didn't.

He was to be immortal. This was only a mistake, I thought. A few details come back. I find no order in them.... Whoever fixed his head didn't get the flap of his temple to lie flat. And his wife was too loud in church, assuring her father over and over again that were it not for my brother she would never have known gentleness. It was November, raining and foggy in the grey winter. My mother and father and I joined hands and walked across the other graves. I keep seeing a photograph of us. I keep thinking we were three figures in a Greek frieze, moving in slow motion over the other graves. And then a blackness settled in...a blackout. A series of photographs as if we were holding up washes to reality.

But lately I've had the feeling—lately I feel I can touch his temples, the silk curls of his carved skull. I still don't know why I loved him so passionately. I think it was only his baby laughter. Because Mama would leave us, and I'd have something useful to do. Once when the old priest came to our house he said, I want to take your baby home. I replied, Go make your own baby. Remember?

We hardly ever talked about our unhappiness as children, about our parents' restless moving. My younger brother had nothing to say. Always afraid, he would stay locked in his room. Maybe I loved him for the hum of his reluctance, something to steady myself. I remember the songs we'd hear on the radio. I could never bring back the actual moving day. I don't know whether there were large moving vans, or if we fled in the night like gypsies. I'm not certain whether I packed my clothes in boxes or luggage. But I'd whistle the radio songs to him as we walked into the oaky mosses of Mississippi. I'd sing, "You are my lucky star," and his hair would glow like sunshine. Or "All I do is dream of you the whole night through," and he'd open his eyes wide.

On the empty, windswept desert of my memories of him, just a few gestures return, a few vignettes sparkle like silvery water. My father was always riding the crest of the oil business in those days. Always drinking. I was ten, my brother five. Somehow we managed to land in a house with Bea, whose real name was Beatrice. She was a poet who never left us. Mother said we needed her cooking, but we wanted her there all the time. "Bea, Bea," we'd call—you were too young for school, and often mother forgot to take me. Bea would appear at our bedroom door, reciting *The Rime of the Ancient Mariner*: "O there was an ancient mariner," she'd begin. And we would all take turns. That would be enough. Then my brother and me flipping through the Army/Navy catalog: everything on this page is yours, everything on that one is mine.

Later—ages twelve and seven I think—we lived in an older house, stone maybe, few windows, in Gulfport, with grey overarching oaks and green moss in the front. I never knew why the black butterflies circled our bougainvillea: they seemed uncommon, more like vultures than butterflies. And the ants, they too were unreal. I still don't remember their stings, just my brother's spindly legs, all the baby fat gone, all bones in a white sunsuit. Orphans. My shorts blood-red—he said, "fire engine," but I knew better. The surface of the Gulf lay rippling and warm. We'd wade out first, barely missing the grey mucous jellyfish undulating like underwater butterflies. Then he'd pick up the bucket, impatient to be off. Standing on the warm wood of the pier, we'd lower our own fishing strings, ignoring the clear balloons with their ugly liquid. The wood would be warm. We'd lower our strings, and they'd hold on! Do crabs have teeth? he'd ask. Fat and coral-colored, they would clench the string all the way up! We'd be fair, placing them on their stomachs so they could scuttle a bit. Then we turned them over, their claws furiously waving. I'd rub their stomachs, and they'd sleep. Later my father's friend said we lied, that we couldn't have done it without bait. Paralysis was impossible.

It was really our obeisance to Mother, Mother emblazoned in her innocence, our blue diaphanous princess waiting for us as if it were nothing to find two ragged minions standing at the back door, crabs still slopping in a bucket of seawater. I loved my mother then. I remember her and Bea in the kitchen with pots of boiling water and spices.

Then I lost him. He looked away. When the soldier on another beach—blocks away from the butterflies and the boiling crabs—asked me to play jumpfrog with him under water, his fingers gentle but steady, I never told Mother. But my brother looked away after that. I lost him. He...when mother and I...the trips to the dressmakers, the move back to Louisiana, I was to dance they said, I would marry one day. At the dressmaker's—once the dressmaker's son watched her pin up my chiffon hem. "Mother, why does he slobber?" I would ask. Somehow out of kilter—Mother now in her fox fur. "People have deficiencies," she'd say. Don't stare at the dressmaker's son. Somehow out of kilter. My brother hated my developing breasts as much as I did. Once we stood at the top of the stairs. "Everyone in this house wants you to die." His voice choked with shame. He hated his own lust for me. His hands shook with attraction. He chased me...down—down—down...and that was all.... There were marriages, but we were deaf to their eruptions. There were tears, but the water ran back into our brains, calcifying their subtle ridges with salt until he could no longer stand the rigidity. He was twenty-three when he shot himself.

❖❖❖

Calvin devours all that is put before him at breakfast. *Croissants, pain au chocolat.* "More *crème*, little

Mia!" he shouts. "More *café au lait!*" I want it to be regular. Like before. People get up, and sometimes there's coffee and talk. Sometimes people talk. They're careful about too much sugar, but they talk. I no longer eat very much. I've become too aware of my throat mechanism. This morning there are two lamps with green shades projecting light onto the oval table. Calvin has placed a white piece of paper right in the center. I try to fix it with my eyes so I won't float outside of it. But when I sit down, the paper seems to slide, the table arches like waves overreaching toward some elusive conclusion. It's okay, this life of movement. The clear green grass sways. I'm wearing my clean green shirt again and the contours of my face are exactly the same—and the table was once a tree. When I get back to my room, I'm going to write a note to Cecilia:

> I'm so hidden here by this dark uncertain kingship. I'm not sure you can see me any more.

"I've got good news, Elizabeth—life!" says Calvin. The jackhammers have already begun there in the front....

"Why don't you ask me about my past, Calvin?" Calvin's quiet. I've never seen him so quiet.

"I want to know about your past, but now you need more outside activity. The patient needs company first, writing second. Mia, give her the *chèvre*. She's pale!"

I refuse it. It's not food I want. It doesn't work to swallow. But the novel seems far away, like somebody else made up a plot and handed it to me, a plot I no longer like.

"First you'll meet people with connections. No wonder you don't write. You don't know anyone!"

"What people? I was writing yesterday morning and Mia interrupted me!"

"I'm so sorry. Forgive me for sending her in."

"It doesn't matter; it was another's writing I wanted...." I'm suddenly aware of his gaze.

"I'm preparing a dinner, my dear, kind of an artistic Parisian début—but done in good taste! These guests will be the right sort of people, people with the right connections for you. Just believe in yourself."

"Who are they, then? What should I believe?"

"I know this is difficult for someone like you, a professor..."

"Not the kind of professor they wanted."

"And quite right! You're an artist."

With one swift slice, Calvin slides the white paper to the front of my empty plate.

"You're the artist! Here's your list of patrons. There'll be Madame and Monsieur Sichot, both stockbrokers, connected to Gallimard, the best publishers. There'll be Monsieur Michael Dreyfus—you'll like him—an architect with enlightened opinions about student unrest. There'll be—"

"What opinions?"

"Michael's sympathetic with student ideals, but skeptical about their methods."

"I've been reading the papers about those students—"

"Quiet, Elizabeth—you know nothing, just nothing about French politics."

"I know what's happening in Berkeley. And we

believe that the war in Vietnam is the most immoral America has ever—"

"Why didn't you stay there, then, with your damned Communists?"

"Because of her...because I had to get away ."

"Because of whom?"

"Because I had to get away, that's all...I had nothing...."

"Nothing's wrong—you'll write. You'll see how I've prepared a house for you..."

"Calvin, I don't know the language! How can I speak to them?"

"But Calvin is ready for all your contingencies, my sweet!"

"I'm not your 'sweet' ."

"I'm sorry. I'm just joking. I'm just a discarded old man, not sensitive enough for you new women! I'll start again. I've engaged a private tutor for you. A man called Julien. He's competent—appropriate for someone of your stature."

Part Three

Julien

8

Julien is not my brother, I know he's not, though he has the same delicate carved skull, the same curly hair. My brother's gone to another place. Still, when Julien walks toward the dining room that first day, I want to tell him the story of Mary Magdalene because I feel like her when I see him—how Mary, supposing Jesus to be the gardener who stood at the door of the sepulchre, said, "If you have taken him away, tell me." How when she recognized him, she tried to take his hand, saying, "My body still carries the imprint of your body and now I have found you again!" But he replied, "Go work in the world—go fight in the streets for the right-eous, and tell them that nothing is forbidden if you have seen me."

When Julien sits down to listen to the radio, he motions me to join him.

"I want to become competent, Julien. I need to make appointments. I can't even use the telephone."

"Have you had lessons before?"

"I learned to *read* some French for my Ph.D., but I've lost most of it."

"Calvin said I should prepare you for his dinner party...I can tell you want other things...."

"I'd like to know something about *you*, about my language teacher."

"There is not a lot to tell. I started teaching English at the Berlitz School when I was nineteen. Now I work at the Alliance Française and do many private jobs. I've translated medical journals for Calvin."

"Where'd you do your university work?"

"I was not educated beyond the *lycée*. So you see, you are superior to your teacher."

There's something blessed in Julien's manner. A quietness and a depth. Without even trying, he seems to be the kind of man who can walk into a room and make one happy.

"I want to break this silence, Julien, I've *got* to break it."

"Yes, I promise you we will. We'll accomplish a lot. Each day I'll begin with the workbook and then switch to the radio. That ought to help you hear how people actually talk."

I love his efficiency, his sweetness. He's like a young monk, entering a serene fifteenth-century monastery. I'll pretend to be a brilliant boy from the provinces, a French orphan learning his grammar for the first time, I think. This is not Calvin's home at all, but a cool, light hall with a long pine table where the two of us sit calmly to talk. No longer the shallow elegance of a mahogany table. No longer the emptiness.

Handing me the Alliance Française workbook, he says, "The French engender their articles *and* their pronouns. The English word "a" is an indefinite article. But in French the indefinite article *une* goes with a feminine noun and the indefinite article *un* accompanies a masculine noun. Observe."

une fille intelligente
un garçon blond.

"You've just reversed the usual," I laugh.

"Uh, huh! You're intelligent, Elizabeth, but I'm just a blond!"

"I like this lesson!"

"Well, the pronouns aren't so subversive! The subject pronoun *il* is masculine and the subject pronoun *elle* is feminine. But when both masculine and feminine nouns are the subject, *ils* is used as the subject pronoun. Okay? Read this."

Paul et Marie France sont élèves
but
ILS
sont amis

"Why?" I ask.

"Because *ils* is understood to be the universal! Sexism is so repulsive."

"But I thought you were Calvin's—"

"Rubber stamp? No, he's just misjudged me. What about you?"

This teacher Julien is not my brother but his possibility, his newness—the flower connected to the earth, and out of the sky a clear lip of water, the drip of rain on our fingertips, gaily opening the red umbrellas. Perhaps there are no journeys from which we can't return. My brother always moving toward the light.

"I don't know—I'm not his rubber stamp, but I'm not thankless either. If it weren't for his help in Fuveau..."

I've read this story before, I think. How I'd rather be sick and with Cecilia than well and away....How I'm looking for a framework in which to enclose myself. How I'm afraid of not knowing how to diagnose myself...

"I understand," Julien responds.

"Separation is hard for me now, that's all. I was going to find a place to rent, but somehow it seems so useless. This was going to be temporary, but now I don't have the courage to leave him. I *will* make some changes soon, when I get money from the United States. When I want your help, can I ask you?"

"Of course, you know you can. Just don't wait too long." Julien turns up the radio and stands. Through the static comes a perfect Parisian accent. Julien translates the broadcaster's words for me.

"Today twenty American aircraft bombed Nam Dinh in the Kamau peninsula. Each air carrier carried six thousand pounds of bombs. Five used napalm. North Vietnamese women and children tried to take cover under mimosa trees. Thousands were killed. Others, hit by napalm, ran into the river."

I see him cover one hand with another. His eyes look away as if he can't stand to face me.

"What are we listening to, Elizabeth? How can I teach French when this brutality is going on?"

"Children—just victims of chance. It must be so frightening...."

"The political idiots of America tell the American people that they alone are capable of freeing Vietnam.

It's like the egotism of a stupid giant, stepping everywhere without looking!"

I see Julien tremble with resentment.

"The French students are sick of that kind of egotism, aren't they?" I say. "Sick of the class system. Sick of failing before they have a chance."

"Che Guevara predicted this revolution a year ago when he spoke at the Tricontinental Conference."

"What did he say?"

"He talked about outsiders and the young—how tired they are of the Communist Party's tepid organizing. He said the only revolutionary thing to do was rely on our own selves without expecting others to take care of us. Then he was ambushed and killed in Bolivia. Taken off by helicopter to *Valle Grande.* God, the terror of it!"

"I'm so lonely for a good world, Julien, for the twentieth century everyone wanted."

"I'm sure other people feel that way too—a loneliness for a *good* world, not a world built on lies and hypocrisy—"

Julien is my political ally. He's almost like a brother to me. Maybe I'll find myself over here, I think. Know that my body works—has solidity—that I can depend on myself.

Over the next week I start to trust Julien because he's begun to confide in me. We go over the terrible broadcast time and time again. We curse the Vietnam war. Sometimes he teases me.

"Why don't I ever see you in jangly earrings and leather boots like the other Paris hippies wear?"

"Because I'm not as free as they are, and the war's more serious than that."

I get the impression his life is hemmed in, limited

to teaching and reading. For some reason, perhaps because he knows I'll go away soon, he's really talking to me, asking something of me. It took five days for Julien to admit he had a sister. She was an epi-leptic, he said. One evening, when he was two, and she was eight months old, his mother and father left their small apartment in the quartier *Tolbiac* to attend their nephew's bar mitzvah. They asked a young woman from the neighborhood to stay for three hours. Apparently he was sick with a sore throat, and the young woman left the baby to care for Julien—just for a few minutes. When she returned, the baby had gagged on her own tongue. Julien's parents removed everything from the baby's room, and never spoke of her again.

"When I was sixteen, I went to a psychic," he said. "I told her I had never touched a girl...I thought something was wrong. She said I had lost someone very close to me years and years ago."

"Were you afraid?"

"Just determined."

"When did you find out?"

"For a year, I asked my mother questions. Finally one night, she took pity on me. I was studying English verbs when she told me the truth. I left the next day. I still see my parents on holidays."

"Oh, Julien. What a tragic loss."

"Yes. Sometimes I find sisters, but never lovers."

So we work on our verbs, and together we read passages from Debray's *Revolution in the Revolution*. I repeat to myself over and over again, "I am a child of God, I am a worthwhile person." I pray that Julien will be happy some day. I practice my French regularly. Maybe I'll meet some students soon. One day at lunch, I tell Julien about how afraid I am of Calvin.

"I dread Calvin's dinner party, Julien. He thinks if I meet influential conservatives, I'll start writing! *Calvin donne une fête, mais Elizabeth écoute un disque.*"

"Good! Do what you wish," he says.

"*Pendant la fête, je vais écouter un disque de jazz—* in my bedroom," I finish hopefully. "*Il n'est pas du tout difficile,*" I add.

We both smile. "*C'est merveilleux!*"

My French is improving. But will I really do what I've said—listen to records in my room during Calvin's party? I see Julien look at me wistfully. I think, maybe in another life....

When the dinner finally takes place, Laurence Sichot and his wife are the first to enter Calvin's uncomfortable dining room. Monsieur Sichot is balding and she, a retired stock-broker like her husband, appears agitated. Neither of them speak to me. They talk interminably about the skills involved in conservative investing. Monsieur Sichot finishes his rare beefsteak and launches into his favorite subject. "The students at Nanterre are despicable. Roving bands of them, mainly Trotskyists, came into the city and attacked the American Express office on rue Scribe today. Protesting the Americans' retaliation against the Tet Offensive."

Calvin bristles. "Let them stick to their protests against dormitory regulations and stop attacking the Americans! Vietnam is already infected with Communism!"

I feel an anger in my stomach. "The Americans are using napalm. The Communists don't do that!"

"Elizabeth, my dear, would you have the United States become like Canada? Completely without weapons, completely without power? Everyone argues that Third World countries should govern themselves, but the South Vietnamese can't do it alone."

I look away in fury.

"Hell, Elizabeth, aren't you aware that the greatest masters of red-baiting in France are the Communists themselves? Not only have they not supported the student leader Daniel Cohn-Bendit, they've labeled him as a dangerous participant in an international conspiracy!"

"Calvin..."

"Your political beliefs have no reality! It's too absurd. These young whipper-snapper professors are nothing but civil servants! And they're trying to overthrow the Government which allows them all the liberties they enjoy! And the fashionable intellectuals like Sartre, Foucault and Lacan! They're even worse!"

Calvin's architect friend Michael shifts uneasily in his chair. "Why don't you and I continue this debate?"

"Michael," Calvin says, "there's a rumor going round. The lunatic students at the École *des Beaux Arts* are planning a massive strike. Some posters already up picture a damned suffocated student with the word *Réformes* at the top and *Chloroforme* at the bottom. And all over the Sorbonne slogans saying, *Il est interdit d'interdire* confuse everybody."

I savor the slogan: It is forbidden to forbid.

"What's their complaint?" Michael asks.

"They're berating their dons and the Order of the Architects. Your sort of folks. They're claiming there are three deaths every day in the building industry. Class consciousness. That sort of thing."

"Why do the young continue to exaggerate?" Michael looks shyly at me.

Calvin winks. "The French know what to do with revolts. Best to let the uprising ripen, give them lots of leeway, hope for excesses, wait for public opinion to swing against them, and then come down hard on them!"

"Behold the new Machiavelli!" Michael laughs.

"But Mia will take us away from our vulgar arguments, won't you, my luscious chef? Time now for the *crème caramel* and coffee."

Turning to me, Calvin says, "Tell our friends how we read together each evening—piecing together the legends of Montparnasse. Tell them..."

I think of the terrible broadcast, of Julien's outrage, see a river eating away inevitably at the land's edge with great precision. But Jesus said to Mary Magdalene, "Go work in the world—go fight in the streets for the righteous, and tell them that nothing is forbidden if you have seen me."

"No—I've read something today more relevant than legends of the poets of Montparnasse. I'm sure all of you knew about the Basilique de St. Denis—where all the French kings and queens were buried. When the Revolution broke out, the mobs stormed the church and sacked it. Opened all of the coffins and stole everything worth taking. They dumped all of the bones into common pits. They're still sorting the toes and legs! This should interest you, Michael. Notre Dame was modeled on St. Denis."

Calvin's friends clap and smile.

"Elizabeth is living through a political period, but culture is the activity we hold in common. Now it's my turn, and I'm *not* bored with poetry and legendary poets!"

Calvin never takes his eyes off my face. "Apollinaire

was struck down by poverty—as many of our great artists are," he begins. "And to support himself, he spent entire days in the Bibliothèque Nationale examining licentious texts! What work, eh, Michael? His friend Ferdinand Fleuret helped him edit fourteen volumes of the stuff! Can you imagine what it would entail to assemble a critical bibliography of pornography for the Bibliothèque Nationale, Elizabeth? Well, he did it and it remains the definitive reference work to this day!" His laugh is low and lilting, like a girl's.

    I'll leave the house more often now, I think. Be with children—perhaps the Jardin des Plantes and the Jardin d'Acclimation. As the guests hurry home, I lock the door of my bedroom.

9

Driving, driving now away from the house, away from the blue satin bedroom, I look at Calvin as if he were an older brother. Was there an older brother? Did we live for years together in a white house by the sea? Most of my memory is intact. But not everything. Calvin claims I'm in a state of forgetfulness because of my sadness, because of my hypoglycemia.

Today Calvin's silver Citroën feels like a smoothly cantering horse. His straight black hair is like the mane of a thoroughbred. Calvin has packed pâté sandwiches and strawberries in a lovely wooden picnic basket. I wonder if I'll ever write again.

"We will have lunch beside the lake and the lake will absolve us," he says.

"Do we need absolution?" I ask.

"Oh, we all have troublesome pasts." He laughs uneasily.

As we drive into the bois de Boulogne, I feel that Calvin cares for me. Here is my friend, and I have been too selfish to see him. I begin to awaken a little from the dead permanent days—has it been two weeks?

three? Is it possible that the house exchange fell through after all my planning? Perhaps I'll go back to Fuveau. I could manage that. Is it possible that the house exchange was a figment of my imagination?

Calvin and I walk into the park; the tears are brimming in his eyes. I know nothing of his young life. Was there an unrequited love, or the death of a beloved fiancée? Or has Calvin always been this dark, harsh orphan? Why do we never really know?

As we walk toward the mare St.-James, the filtered noon air wraps the river into sudden sapphires of water. Young women in bright blue jerseys bicycle past, and I feel my heart beat like a butterfly's wings. I've felt these wings beating within me before.

"It seems that these vast wooded pines and water lilies have mastered the art of waiting," I say.

"Yes," Calvin replies. "These natural surroundings are good for you." And for a time, we balance on a silent plateau of rest. This is Calvin's gentler side, I think.

"Elizabeth," Calvin says, "you're much too thin for a young woman your age. You're built more like a boy than a girl." Calvin reaches out to touch my hips, but quickly withdraws his hand.

"I am just a naturally thin person," I argue.

Turning abruptly, I see the wild irises nodding happily beside the sapphire lake. I dream of an earlier time, when my mother and I canoed through some silken waters—wasn't it in Arkansas? She'd take the bow position and I'd maneuver the stern. We'd carry big packages of potato chips and roast beef sandwiches. She was afraid of the water by herself, but never with me.

"Why did you insist on being petulant last night?

Why did you ignore Michael? Don't you know he's one of our leading architects?"

I hesitate. "I don't know what to say to your friends. They look at me as if I'm insane. As if I were visiting you only briefly from a dark asylum. Michael is no different from the rest."

"You're so self-pitying, Elizabeth. You're so self-indulgent. I'm giving you the best Paris has to offer...."

My heart heaves up a familiar sadness. Better to live alone. Better to die alone, away from his hatred. I must find a way to escape him. I must find my house.

"Let's not snarl at each other, my little sweetheart. We should do something fun before I return to my work. The Fleuriste Municipale and the Jardin d'Acclimation? You choose."

His firm lips are so full of determination. My anger evaporates like the vapor in the sunny sickrooms of early childhood.

"I haven't played for such a long time. How about the Jardin d'Acclimation?"

As we walk into the amusement park, I stare with wonder at the thin, energetic Frenchwomen pushing their sleeping babies in elegant white prams.

"Perhaps when your health becomes more stable, we'll find you an appropriate husband and, who knows, maybe you'll be pushing a pram in the Bois de Boulogne, too."

"Calvin, stop patronizing me! I'm not your daughter and I'm leaving you soon."

Calvin glares at his pocket watch and reaches for a cigarette. I sense his fury.

"I respect your time, Calvin. Why don't you just leave me here by La Musée de l'Herbe and come back for me in three hours?"

His hands shake as they light the cigarette. He's going home to drink. Always, always in the late afternoon.

"Yes, so kind, so kind. My clever little patient, so considerate of her doctor's brilliant career!"

I stare at Calvin's blue cotton sweater and his elegant long legs until I can see he has crossed the street and is disappearing into a sea of Renaults and Citroëns. I want to run after him, want him to hold my hand, to assure me that he hasn't meant to be unkind. But I force myself to stop.

I'll buy ice cream and some Perrier, then walk over to the Municipal Garden and smell the amber-pink roses. I'll sit under the mimosa trees. I'll just be quiet and look at the trees and then go back to the amusement park. But I can't help noticing a tiny woman who sits on a park bench throwing bits of chocolate éclair at the noisy pigeons pecking around her patent leather shoes. First she feeds the pigeons, and then she taps her right foot as if preparing to stand up and dance. Her childlike behavior is only enhanced by her blond, curling, bushy hair which frames her heart-shaped face. Her blue eyes rimmed in green are astonishingly young.

I stand spellbound as this woman opens her artist's portfolio and begins looking at her paintings. Moving to a park bench beside her, I glance at the portfolio. There at the top I see a shockingly violent and yet tender image. A young surgeon listens with his stethoscope to the heart of a dead man he's pulling up out of a deep, black grave. The dead man must be the surgeon's twin! Dirt and dry ivy vines fly to the periphery of the painting, making it hard to discern whether or not the corpse-like twin is beginning to smile as the doctor pulls him to a sitting position atop the dry dirt. Are the doctor and the dead man the same? I must have this woman for a friend. But why would she be interested in me?

There's a shadow behind me. It's a tall blond man, a modern Rip Van Winkle who speaks to the artist with an Afrikaaner accent.

"You are a talented young woman," he says, standing very straight as if saluting a colonel. He hands her his card. "Melvin Grandstone: Undertaker, Johannesberg, South Africa," he says. "I can't claim the exalted status of doctor, but I do my share to help the world turn," he says. "Tell me about yourself."

"I'm Colette," she says haughtily. "I study painting at the École des Beaux Arts."

She tries to continue, but is interrupted by the blond man's laughter.

"Don't *you* lie to me," he is suddenly stern. "Colette was a writer and a femme fatale. You are hardly more than a girl."

"And you are a pissant," she says.

A tremor of excitement shoots through my chest.

"Look, we've started off all wrong," he apologizes. "I just want to buy that picture for my father. He's a podiatrist!"

"And does he raise people from their graves?" she sneers.

"How can you claim to be an artist," he continues, "when you are so careless about your manners?"

"I won't sell you this picture!" She shoves it back in her portfolio and walks away from him.

He rushes after her, cursing her for her rudeness and making ridiculous offers.

"I'm offering you 60 francs, you ungrateful upstart."

I jump to my feet and run to Colette's side.

"Hello Colette—sorry I'm late! Who's this criminal? Shall we call the police?"

Colette quickly takes up the pretense. "First the police and then the American Embassy. I'm sick of these bums!"

"I'm asking only that we do business," he says. "Is there a law against—"

"This doctor is a member of our family, and this painting celebrates his heroism." My resourcefulness surprises me.

"A goddamned *family* of dilettantes," he mutters and walks away.

Colette throws her head back with laughter, exposing the curve of her throat. I'm exhilarated to be standing next to such a bold woman.

"So you're a painter?" I begin.

"Yes, and whoever you are, you're sharp as hell! Come on. I'll treat you to a café au lait."

As we sit down at the white wrought-iron round table, I see the green leaves swirl in the afternoon wind. I feel a golden filament of sun drawing me into the gaiety of Colette's cobalt eyes.

Colette brushes a leaf from my summer coat. "And who are you, my beautiful one?"

I blush. "I'm the patient of a prominent internist in Paris. Beyond that I'm searching for a calling—I think. Elizabeth O'Connor is my name."

"How super to be cared for by someone who's prominent! My father walked out when I was twelve. I began working in a tomato cannery that summer."

"Where were you living?" For a minute I have this fantasy that she grew up close to me.

"We lived in Corpus Christi. Mother's still there. Poor darling! All those Navy men who look like constipated penguins, and the dumb blond body builders. If I had the money I would live a nomad's life."

"Don't you do that now, Colette? Traveling round the world as a painter?"

"No, I have to prove myself. I have to finish my training at the École des Beaux Arts. I live in a seedy part of town—Dausmenil—share the rent with a guy named Jacques. It's platonic...and dull."

Looking up at the swallows overhead, Colette says, "I would like to migrate every year, as they do."

She looks as if she should be standing on the steps of a cara-van surrounded by pots and pans and half-mended tables....Catching a glimpse of the red leotard beneath her black silk blouse, I feel strangely excited and a little afraid.

"Are you a dancer?" I ask.

"Yes, I dance several nights a week at a very posh place, not far from here. Supports my life as an artist!" She laughs, but turns away to avoid my eyes.

She is so courageous, and I'm nothing but a neurotic has-been. She's on some journey to a star, I think. Like a child running through silver olive groves talking to the birds.

"Is it more dangerous to be afraid of danger or to live through it?," she asks. "What do you believe? I've been asking all my friends that question."

I look away, focus on a young French girl dressed in brown jodhpurs and a black velvet hard hat, who is cantering her quarterhorse through the silent pines. I dream of riding with the girl far away over the vast expanses of the Persian plains. When I see Colette again her entire face is looking at me. That question is so irrelevant! That question has nothing to do with me.

"Elizabeth," Colette continues. "What frightened you? I don't care whether you answer my silly question."

"The question upsets me—that's all."

Colette explodes with laugher. "I'm searching for bold people, and you're caving in on me!"

There's an uneaten peach at the table. Some careless idiot just left it there. I feel nauseated and angry. Colette's too crass and not to be trusted. She knows nothing about my bravery, how I fought that sexist university and finally got tenure ... how I struggled to say what needed to be said about Djuna Barnes and Thelma Wood in my biography. And she can't know how I defended my brother when Daddy attacked him for his shyness. After three Scotches, my father would slap his face and say, "Let's see what kind of man you are, boy!" I should go home to Julien and become proficient in the language. There will be other friends.

When I look up, Colette has begun a sketch. "I'm doing satire today. I've started a spoof on Rodin's *Burghers of Calais.* You see I've drawn them as women who strut rather than suffer."

She's an artist *and* a feminist. I can't lose her!

"We'll become good friends, won't we, Colette? This will be more than a chance meeting, won't it? I live on the Rue Froidevaux in Montparnasse. Will you remember?"

"Yes, of course we'll become friends! I may need you as a witness to our Mr. Grandstone!" And once again, the features of Colette's face are like green jewels, and there is a settling of the leaves, and for a moment I remember the season of fall and new beginnings.

"Why don't you come to my art school, Elizabeth! We've been on a strike since May 8. My friends and I started the Atelier Populaire, a group that laughs at the Order of Architects and denounces the idea that art is sacred. Come tomorrow to paint signs with us for the revolution. The École des Beaux Arts is on the corner of rue Bonaparte and the Quai Malaquais. You make only two Métro changes from your house."

"I *want* to, Colette. It will be the first time I've gone a long way from my doctor's house alone. I live with my doctor now. You think I can do it?"

"Sure you can!"

And then everything's moving at the periphery, just beyond the cedar trees. The music is a slow, melancholy crescendo of violins. And the violins are hovering over two women in a room with blue irises and white chairs. I can almost see her face, and she is calling, "Elizabeth, Elizabeth!" Suddenly I recognize Calvin's voice, sodden drunk and calling me. Lurching up the path toward La Musée de l'Herbe, he sings a hymn, something like "Rock of Ages, Cleft for Me."

Turning to Colette, I ask for her telephone number. "I must run, you see. I've neglected my watch. We've planned cocktails with a Paris broker...."

"I'll see you tomorrow, and one day I'll meet your brilliant doctor," Colette says. Quickly copying her number, I run in the direction of La Musée de l'Herbe.

Part Four

Colette

10

I stand at the window in Paris as the day begins to open, and the little milk trucks clamor through the sleeping streets. I watch my reflection in the hazy golden pane, and know that soon, in three hours to be exact, I've agreed to meet Colette at the École des Beaux Arts. She is so fabulous, this Colette. If Julien is right, the Friday street fairs should be in full swing today. He's given me Métro and bus schedules and red gaudy street maps for "smart navigation," he says. I think I'll walk round this city of wonder today—try to see it as Julien does. The underground can wait. To my disappointment, though, there are no street vendors outside my door as I abandon Calvin's house at 8 a.m.

"Remember," Julien said, "you have to leave the fancy neighborhoods like Montparnasse and roam the little streets." And what could be smaller and more intriguing than the rue Mouffetard? Just the sound of it pleases me. The thought of that one street makes me want to explore. So I gather my sandwiches and walk out the door.

The boulevard St.-Michel is the direct route. It leads you to the river, if nowhere else. I can't get lost if I can see the Seine! Signs of the revolution are everywhere, in street windows and plastered on the bumpers of old cars. In the big student bookstore on the boulevard St.-Michel, a clamorous red poster says:

The Boss Needs You
You Don't Need Him.

And across the street in a mechanic's *atélier*, another sign reads, *"Brisons les Vieux Engrenages,"* Let's Break the Old Cogs.

I'm going to have breakfast in the rue Mouffetard, I think, and if I can find a fair I'll buy a white pear and a bottle of red wine for Colette's lunch. As I approach the choked boulevards and impassable side streets near the Panthéon, I see a Friday street fair raging in the courtyard at Place Monge. Cabbages, pears, cauliflowers, apples, enormous leeks, potatoes, almonds, and oranges stand gleaming in bright metal sheds all over the courtyard. Stopping for a pear, I see the cardboard bins with their myriads of used sweaters and dresses. Closer to the rue Mouffetard, entire chickens hang with feathers still fluffy and eyes still open. The sellers are screaming, "Choucroute and sausage. Come buy your dinner here!"

Time to turn in the direction of the river. Lord, how the sun comes in like a flood. Strolling lovers, oblivious to the glittering waters, kiss and cling to one another. I look away, hurry on. For the longest time nothing moves along the river, yet slowly one barge and then another move away from moorings and lumber down the river as if the weight of the Cathedral were no longer heavy enough to hold them from their sacred adventures.

The Quai des Grands Augustins is the oldest one in Paris, or so a beautiful bronze placard tells me. And I can imagine the medieval colors, the indigo hundreds of years ago, slathered across the circular spires in the Great Augustine Monastery which *was* here. And the indigo today becomes the waters where the silk jackets of beautiful women flutter in the winds. All this fluttering and bursting of the moorings seems a good sign for a Friday morning. The quays lined with their mosaic of red and purple bookstalls parade before me.

The École des Beaux Arts itself began as a monastery when a woman, Marguerite of Valois, founded it in 1608 and dedicated it to the prophet Jacob. Maybe she, the first wife of Henry IV, was so afraid of her husband that she had to do something to justify her life. I suppose there are always people who speak from their prisons about inexplicable freedoms. It's their words, their buildings, that continue to pierce us with uncomfortable illuminations.

Only a cloister and a small church remain from the original monastery. At 14 rue Bonaparte, I turn into a courtyard, then up the ornate pink stairs to the École des Beaux Arts. Once inside, it's another century, the one I live in, at least for the moment. Colette's watching for me. Her long black leotard is covered with an enormous blue plastic apron, which is splattered with scarlet and gold.

Everybody's working here, everybody's laughing. A boy holds a frame on which a girl stretches silk.

"Art should be anonymous," she says.

"Or at least a collective effort," he replies.

The robust posters of Atelier Populaire of the École des Beaux Arts. Some of the posters are finished and propped against the wall. They try to admonish us, the already converted, to action:

> "Mankind will not live free until the last capitalist has been hanged with the entrails of the last bureaucrat."

> "Every view of things which is not strange is false."

Julien keeps telling me something I can't forget: he says we are what we put up with. I'm beginning to look at what I've endured all these years—and to question it.

Colette's got to understand that I'm growing stronger. She's got to see that I'm intelligent about this political situation, too, so she'll care about me.

"There's some gossip," she says, leading me to an easel. "Some Citroën workers have come up to Paris to debate the intellectuals. Our student buddies! They talk about coalition and what will happen at the Odéon this Friday. We could sit with the students."

"Yeah—I want to, but I'm more at ease with the Americans...their Zen...even their marijuana."

"Yesterday, I saw some of your American hippies near the Panthéon. Should I go buy you the guy with long black hair, carrying the sign which says 'Cleanliness is the luxury of the poor. Be dirty'?"

"I'd like it better if she were a girl with short black hair!"

She's giggling, her brilliant eyes throw a light over

the tireless students. I'm starting to reach her now. If only we'd met in America, before we both...if only Colette had been the one, not Cecilia.

"What slogan should we use for our next poster? How about 'The Struggle Continues'?"

"Yes, it does! But my heart's so weary. I don't know what to do about Calvin."

"You told me he was a great doctor! What's happening, Elizabeth?"

"He's a retired doctor. I've only known him three weeks. He's often angry with me."

"Where'd you meet him?"

"In Fuveau, in southern France!"

"Oh, one of *those* meetings!"

"No, nothing like that. I made a house exchange. But there was never a house in Fuveau."

"Did you have the right address? Haven't you contacted the person in your house?"

"I don't want to talk to anyone in Berkeley yet. I may never go back there."

Colette looks relaxed, as if she's heard now what she needs to hear.

"I understand about doctors. Jacques is an intern at the Pasteur Institute. Sometimes he's terrible, too."

"We've got that in common, anyway. Calvin taught there. But something's wrong. I think something shocking happened to him years ago. When he looks at me there's a blank silver look to his eyes."

"So you met him in Fuveau?"

"Yes. I was really down. I couldn't find the house I was supposed to live in. I didn't know anyone."

"Maybe it was the right address in the wrong village. Maybe there was a miscommunication."

"Could be. But Calvin was all I had. He was there

and I was exhausted and nervous from the trip. I'm hypoglycemic...my condition has been bad. He offered me a place to stay in Paris, and some treatment."

"What's he done, other than take you in?"

"He never leaves me alone. He hates my appearance, but he's always touching me, always telling me I'm too thin. And when he drinks, he mistakes me for his daughter, Renée. He says, 'Renée, let's get out the bicycles and ride to the moon....' Then I pity him. That's the trouble. Sometimes he sits outside my door at night and stares at the floor...all night long."

"Do you want Jacques to check on Calvin's past?"

"Oh, would he help me?"

"He'll do what I say, and I say we're going to take care of each other! Here, start lettering. This one's going to say, 'Professors, you are old!'"

Colette smiles at me with her delicate mauve lips. I'm intrigued with her outrageously innocent eyes. They make me forget...

"Let me tell you a story to get your mind off that asshole. Let me tell you about another asshole, my art history teacher. Monsieur Durand's his name. Pompous, like all the rest of 'em. Well, a few weeks ago, before the strike began, he said the image owes something to the memory. Stupid, stupid theories! I stood up and said, 'How can you talk intellectual trash when there's a revolution going on?'"

"What'd he say?"

"He said, 'Sit down, Colette.' But I didn't. I said, 'The memory's everything. Thank you very much. Take my memory of my first crush on an older girl, Peggy!!' 'Sit down, Colette!' He repeated it and cleared his throat. Do *you* want to hear about Peggy, Elizabeth?"

"Sure I do."

"I can still hear the sounds of her voice. Peggy, my camp counselor. I always went to camp on a scholarship and worked part-time in the kitchen. Anyway, Peggy had tanned thighs and short hair with auburn ringlets. We campers were just plain tormented! There'd be her tennis classes and her ballet. Shit! You wouldn't believe the packages from home. My friends got satin toe shoes with wool protectors. Sissy dancing, I thought. But I was a raging tennis player. 'Peggy, watch my lob. Peggy, see how this backhand lands the ball in the back corner.' I had to be first in everything. But none of it touched her. She'd strut through the cabins to kiss us goodnight. She never stopped at my bed.

"But I devised a plan. Next summer I'd be sixteen—old enough to be her assistant. I *wanted* that. Well, anyway, I got the job! Every afternoon at four, Peggy and I planned our teaching strategies. Our final tournament and all. I used the sessions for seduction. 'That Georgia,' I would say, 'executing her backhand return, writhing like a poisoned cat.' And Peggy would laugh. 'You've got a naughty tongue, Colette.' And, blushing, I would rally with, 'It's got other uses, too, you know!' Then we'd strategize. How to get that tomcat, Georgia, to coordinate her feet. How to force that brainless bird, Betsy, to open her eyes and look at the ball.

"Hell, I manipulated Peggy with all my wiles. 'Don't you think Cynthia looked terrific at the match on Thursday?' But Peggy wouldn't take the bait! 'I was more interested in her serve than her sex appeal, Colette.' And always, after our business I'd invite Peggy for a walk. And she'd say, 'Colette, if we don't keep our hands off each other, can we expect the campers to do the same?' And I'd reply 'But they don't Peggy!' Elizabeth, why are you staring?"

"Nothing. Just a memory. Who won?"

"The Choctaws did. Hands down! Then this other girl's parents arrived two days early. Hounded her about her friend. She was so unstrung she couldn't get her serve right. They left finally, all those sexy girls. We spent four days 'evaluating the term.' That's when I sent her a letter. I slipped it under her pillow, only to find an answer, 'Meet me tonight at 10 by the lake.'

"Her body was like the pliant wood of a silver birch tree. Afterwards we slept by the lake. She woke early, yelling, 'A cobra is crawling towards us. Run!'"

"Whatever came of it, Colette?"

"Oh, not much. She went off to Radcliffe. Majored in psychology. Saw her at Halloween, but she seemed embarassed to tell me she was engaged! 'He's ever so androgynous, Colette,' she said. 'And it won't stop our friendship!' But of course, it did."

"Why don't you come to my house, actually to Calvin's house. Will you visit me, Colette? We'll talk about *our* roles in this revolution. Over lunch."

11

It's misty today in Montparnasse, even at noon. Colette will be capable and quick in the fog. She'll maneuver the twisting stairs, ignore the man selling sunglasses and the noon crowds on the shiny subway crossing the river. Calvin's been pacing back and forth in his study all morning. No one's told him Colette's coming for lunch, but he knows instinctively I'm no longer alone. Lately, whenever I'm around him, I notice his fleshy belly, and the way his adam's apple looks like a turkey's neck. Early this morning, he started in on me.

"Why don't I know your whereabouts any more, Elizabeth?"

"Why should you know them?"

"Paris is like a besieged museum! Those students are a bunch of grumblers, shrugging their shoulders! My guess is you're out there with *them,* probably stuffing *their* envelopes and making coffee for American tramps. You're too sophisticated for that, Elizabeth. You're too sophisticated to wait on hippie men!"

"Sophistication has nothing to do with it. I believe

in their causes. I think we're standing on the edge of a new world, and the old one has to be demolished."

"You! You're like diamonds thrown to the pigs. Write, Eizabeth, about *real* emotions, not the shallow delusional emotions of Daddy's boys who'll run home to Daddy's business the minute the going gets rough."

"I'm not ready to write. Right now, I'm going out in the garden and pick flowers—that's enough!"

So I wait for her, praying that she won't change her mind. The lunch is ready. I fixed a fresh fruit salad and sliced chicken with French bread, last night when Calvin slept. The small table outside is already set with an emerald linen cloth and silver.

But when Colette walks into the garden, she appears startled and dishevelled. Instead of her dance leotard, she wears a thin grey cotton shirt and black woolen trousers which look as if they once belonged to Jacques.

"Hi, Colette. I've picked some roses for our lunch. I'm so glad you're here."

As she turns, I can see tears in her eyes.

"What's wrong?"

"Jacques's mad about money again. He's a pissant about the rent."

"Does he pay the rent?"

"Only temporarily, until my first one-woman show goes up."

I pass her the chicken, but she looks at the garden instead of my food.

"When will it go up?"

"It's just a dream now. I'm not much good today, Elizabeth. I feel like a failure."

"I'm not either, really. Lately, I've been trying to write, but I'm just too distracted. Is Jacques going to search for Calvin's records at the Pasteur Institute? What's Jacques' last name? I don't even know it."

"Jacques's last name is Dusson, and yes, he will search, though he's reluctant."

"Can I pay him for his research, Colette?"

"Oh no! I won't let you!"

"Come on, then. Let's go inside. I want to show you some photographs of Sonia Delaunay over the bed in Renée's mother's room. They're striking."

"Let's do that. Then I have to run. Jacques didn't even want me to leave."

I don't know how to comfort her. Suddenly I make a plunge. "We could live together. If your quartier is inexpensive, why don't you find us a place in Dausmenil?"

"I'll look for *you*. I can't do anything to jeopardize my art."

As Colette is gathering herself to go home, I hear Calvin rush through the bedroom door. He's been listening to us outside the door.

"What's all this about searching for my records? Has Monsieur Dusson lost his mind?"

Colette looks at me, then silently walks past us through the elegant living room and out the door.

"Calvin, must you ruin everything?" I want to kill him.

"You are disrespectful and ungrateful, Elizabeth."

"I have the right to know about your reputation!"

"And I have the right to screen your friends. Who's this Jacques and that hussy, Colette?"

"Jacques is Colette's friend, an intern at the Pasteur Institute, and Colette's an art student! She's a mover and shaker—she participates in the Atélier Populaire. "

"I might have known! Only American trash and French ne'er-do-wells fuel this stupid rebellion."

"But Calvin, did you know there are posters in the courtyard of the Sorbonne, right next to Mao's picture? The whole city supports us now. Red and black Viet Cong flags are everywhere—and the slogans! 'Everything Is Possible.' 'The Imagination Takes Power.' 'Take Your Desires For Realities.' 'It Is Forbidden To Forbid'."

"They're great!"

"They're hogwash! All this taunting of capitalism is just hogwash! The consumer society won't die in France—or America, as far as that goes. These students know nothing about history or the historical evolution of ideas. Liberal democracy is the great leveller, the great destroyer of political upheavals. And it will ultimately destroy this one."

"Daniel Cohn-Bendit wouldn't agree!" I say.

"Daniel Cohn-Bendit is just a hick who hasn't the foggiest notion of political organizing. Hell, even the Communists are ignoring him."

"That's beginning to change! Some Communists have committed themselves to him...."

"Now, Elizabeth, no one can accuse me of anti-Semitism, you know that. But the right wing's got it right this time: carry Cohn-Bendit to the frontier by the scruff of his neck, and end this silly Bolshevik revolution fueled by a few Jews and some silly architects."

"They have a pacifist's passion for violent cleansing! There are thousands of them and their anger keeps me alive! Colette thinks this revolution is bringing me hope."

"My dear, Colette knows nothing about you. You're still delicate, still hypoglycemic."

"Colette thinks I need exercise and anger!"

"Elizabeth, if you take Colette's advice, why don't you take her money, too? You've damned sure taken mine!"

"Lies, Calvin, just lies. I pay for food and transportation. I do nothing...and Colette has no money." His eyes are blazing. How I hate him. Another one to fight.

"Leave me, Elizabeth. You people think I'm going to pay for your girlie girlie lunches—for your girlie girlie slumber parties. I'm thinking of my Renée—who always put *her* art before politics...Mia, is that you at the door?"

As we get up, Calvin shouts, "Go walk in the streets, Elizabeth. You and that whore Colette don't deserve the shelter of my hospitality and wealth."

Part Five

Revolution

12

"Go fight in the streets for the righteous, tell them that nothing is forbidden if you have seen me." May 10, 1968. Friday, Bloody Friday. Colette is teaching me the "Internationale," but here on the boulevard St.-Michel there are no songs, just seas of shuffling feet, maybe thirty thousand, maybe more. The police advance. I am alert for violation. They pull their grey goggles down over their eyes. No one says a word. I've not written one word since our separation. I've trusted no one since Cecilia has gone. The police advance. Their arms move silently, releasing grenades in an uninterrupted arc and then a high hiss of gas and blinding vapor. My feet move back obediently. I am yellow sweat. A heavy smell of rancid metal permeates the air. The students say, "The bourgeoisie will never surrender one iota of power." I see a brown dog run into the gutter. How long can this continue? My eyes feel scalding hot. We've only moved a half inch. We stand in the middle like sandwiches. My mutilated obsessions bleed in pieces on the butcher paper. A hundred yards away the police shove a young French girl in the chest with a rifle butt, while her hands, like furious bees, fly at their faces.

How long can this continue? We move forward again. If I did write to her, my words would be like lost grenades from an old war. She did the best she could—I think. She loved me intensely. In the early days of therapy I sang to her the way Orpheus sang to Eurydice when he led her out of the carnival of death. One day she turned around and stared straight in my face. She realized we were coming into the light and she ran back.

But there were months of ecstasy before that, when my pursuit made each day feel like a wild cantering. Oh, the girlishness of her smile and the heaviness of her breasts! I gave her miniature cars—a German Porsche, an English taxicab. I stretched out my hands to her in the garden, my fingers pointing like a beacon of long gladiolas in the direction of her house. "You can't escape me now," I exclaimed. But I wanted to cry out, "Why did you allow that ritual to happen if you didn't intend—? Our Valentine ritual was everything, a child's ritual, a saturnalia, a marriage. "I bless you forever," you said—with the confetti, thighs touching. We pressed our fingers. "I'll take a clean sharp knife and we'll become sisters," I said. You fed me the Valentine candies—"You can't deny the attraction," I said. "I know the body." "But I would have stopped us," you said. The coarse texture of the hair around your neck, with the rare beauty of things which survive only in part. But you—I could not force the moment—returned to your chair.

"I'm recommending another therapist," you said. "I don't think we should see each other again."

And I dreamt of death by fire, death by pills, death

by the rope that pulls taut. Now I have set myself up in a blue bed, police-locked in Calvin's house, with empty notebooks and cups of tea.

❖❖❖

I'm walking faster now, along with the rest of the crowd. It's as if the French have finally awakened from a long siege of sleepwalking. I'm trying to stay behind a Red Cross truck.

"Wake up, Elizabeth," Colette warns. "We've got to get to a side street. You're mesmerized by this crowd."

"Pull me out of it, Colette. Pull hard, so I don't slip again."

"Push, you little idiot. Don't be afraid!"

I notice the bruises on Colette's arms. Are they a result of today?

Suddenly I want to hit their faces. I hear myself screaming. "What happens next? When we're out of the streets?" What can I say to her? How can I make it right? But they've started to moan and curse. As if in a red phalanx, what seems like a hundred of us shove round a corner and into the rue de la Huchette, the smallest street I've ever seen.

"I'm asking the defenders to stand behind the cars, not on the cars," a male voice blasts over the loudspeaker. Colette and I crouch behind a crushed Citroën. Five hundred yards away, other cars are burning. Smoke smothers my nose. My chest hurts, but I stand up and speak again.

"What about tomorrow, when we're out of the streets?" Someone warns me to duck down.

"There's a wild flag above the barricade—like 1868. What's wrong with you?" Colette asks.

"Not a god-damned thing. Sometimes I just wish the cops would smash my head so I could no longer feel anything for her."

"Who?"

"Cecilia. She was my lover—and my..."

My voice is drowned out. Colette still doesn't know about her.

❖❖❖

"No liberty to the enemies of liberty," some students chant now in the late afternoon. Was she my enemy? Why don't I know? My friend from Berkeley called her unethical. "She did the best she could," I argued. "Think of her as you would any other crutch," my friend insisted. But my world had no form without her.

From a small balcony on rue de la Huchette some old men are screaming, "They're setting fire to Paris!"

"Let them do it!" I say to myself.

You took the easy way—hid in your priest's robes, Cecilia, your fat white hands swishing the soutane. I pitch it now into these street fires. Rather burn with these bombastic French adolescents who pick up their sandals and walk out of their mothers' houses, than end my life in longing..

The defenders of the barricades cover their faces with baking soda and handkerchiefs. Colette flattens her stomach on the pavement.

"Close your eyes—cover them—take off your shirt—anything—we may go blind—" Colette crawls back to the barricade.

Better to be blinded than blind yourself, I think.

"Close your eyes—cover yourself, you idiot. Come here!" Colette holds out her hand.

Suddenly I see the gendarmes' rifles. I see the anger in their bloodshot eyes.

"Colette, I want to fight them! I hate them."

I run back to the barricade, cover my head with a towel thrown from someone's balcony.

❖❖❖

It's 2 a.m. back on the boulevard St.-Germain, and we hear radios blaring. "The students in the Latin Quarter are surrounded. Just a matter of time now."

We lock arms and stand behind our barricades. Colette's forearms are sinewy, like the flanks of young thoroughbreds. The crowd of thousands smells of urine and acid, like trapped horses trying to bolt. The motors grumble toward us. The tanks seem so incongruous. Are they World War II tanks? "Reinforce your positions!" someone screams. We wrap our ankles round each other like anchors in a winter squall. I'm yelling with the others, "Turn your tanks against the bosses, you bastards, you butchers, not us!"

You're the one with no life, Cecilia, not me. You say, "Live your life as you desire. And I'm here in these streets. But you wait for my stories to lift your arms—the jiggle joggle of the wooden puppet. My crayons color the pictures which excite you and release you from that suffocating room where the dramas of incest render your clients mute.

A student near me picks up a hissing grenade to hurl at the gendarmes. Now they are attacking from both sides of the boulevard St.-Germain. Our barricade splinters into fragments of wood, rocks, and rusty car parts as the tanks ram it. We're forced back, falling over each other. I'm afraid I'll faint from lack of air. The hospital orderlies have to dodge the police truncheons to get to the wounded. One captured boy kneels in the street with his hands on his head. The police club him and throw him in their van. Another student walks past, half naked, with his legs lacerated, bleeding, holding his stomach and urinating everywhere.

"We've got to get out now, Colette. I'm choking. My eyes are burning."

"Find an empty flat," she says. "I'm going to vomit. Help me look through the side streets!" But each street to the Sorbonne is crawling with the bastards. Human chains still carry wood, rocks, iron. Bone-weary people in pajamas still make barricades—a three-foot pile of wood, cars, and metal posts. An English terrier with a bleeding ear chews the gendarme's gabardine trousers. Many people, onlookers, just gossip across their tiny balconies as though this were Vietnam.

Up ahead on the rue d'Ulm, police are battering the doors, shouting *"Fermez les fenêtres."* Where the windows remain open, they toss in gas grenades. In a closed flat, I hear a young woman shouting, "I'm pregnant!" And with the bloody thud of a baton, the cop shrieks, "Not anymore you're not!"

Her husband shouts, "We're foreigners!"

"Yes, and you've come to shit on us in France!"

"I'm going in!" I cry. "I'm going to get that woman out!"

"You do and you're dead!" Colette says. "I'm sick. We've got to hide in the Métro. It may run again at dawn!"

I was Cecilia's prisoner. Nothing mattered but those sessions. Her hands were like rose petals on a Japanese silk kimono. I was bound by the silken ropes, and she was toying with me. I'd rather die than live like that. I'd rather kill and be jailed than continue....

13

"I'm continuously astonished at your gullibility, Elizabeth!" Calvin has been slumped in his study, apparently in the same old rocking chair all night, a bottle of Scotch at his feet and a scratchy brown woolen blanket wrapped around his shoulders. Crusts of brown bread and pieces of dry crumbling cheese cover a sheet of stationery with two words on it, "Darling Renée." He looks at me belligerently.

"You and Colette are making coffee and stuffing envelopes for the crassest of hoodlums, people with no respect for private…"

"We don't make coffee for them! We demonstrate alongside them. Some women make coffee. We don't. And they're *not* hoodlums. As for private property, it's the police who…"

"Fuck the police. They didn't help me last night! I was forced to use my revolver…."

I look again at the woolen blanket, now sloshing around Calvin's feet in a pool, where suddenly a black square object snaps into focus. I feel cold.

"Your revolver?"

"Yes. When I heard them jimmying the lock, I ran for my revolver!"

"I don't believe it! They weren't in Montparnasse, were they? Did you shoot at them?"

"Hell, no. I just flushed the covey like a good fox would. Had to put up a show of bravery!"

"I'm leaving, Calvin."

"I'm still dealing with a thankless child!"

"I'm not a child! I'm leaving because of scenes like this." Suddenly I reach for the gun, pulling it to my lap. I've never held a gun. It's smaller than it looked, clammy and cold. It might slip out of my hand if I'm not careful.

You can't keep saving him, some voice intervenes. *But I see him in the stars,* I reply, *his head splitting continuously—from suicide.* The voice drops...

"It's too dangerous, Calvin, for a drunk man to keep a gun...."

"I've beat you to the draw, Elizabeth. *I'm* leaving. I'm not going to be a stranger in my own house now, with that damned Colette around. You've made me old and ugly and unappreciated. All men need *some* respect. You have no respect for your doctor. I curse all women. Take this gun—you'll need it more than I will. I'll teach you to use it."

"Do what you will, Calvin, I'm finding another place."

"Why? Why be so foolish?"

"Because I need to..."

"I'm returning to Fuveau. No need for you to run too. Remember our hotel? It seems like years now. I'll stay there where pimply radicals don't attack the sanctions of private property. Maybe I'll start my memoirs, there among the country people. All I'm asking of you is to watch the house for only a couple of months, until this blows over. They won't attack with you here. I have no other family...."

"But Colette has arranged a rental for me in Dausmenil, near her."

"Let Colette and all her friends come here. It's convenient and comfortable, hell, even elegant! Not that she appreciates elegance."

"Do you *have* to criticize her?"

"Forgive my sarcasm. I'm so distraught."

"Why?"

"I've lost her."

"Who, Calvin?"

"I'm afraid I'll never again see my own daughter. I won't burden you."

"This is the daughter you disinherited. Why?"

"An unfortunate choice on both our parts. I thought I had no choice. She humiliated our family with her choice. And now none of it seems to matter."

"It matters to me! Sometimes I think I see Renée smiling at me. I think she already knows me."

"She *would* smile at you if she were here. I don't know whether she's still alive."

"Hasn't she written to you?"

"Not for years. Not since she was sixteen."

"When did she leave you?"

"I pushed her out over some little girl affair with another girl when she was fifteen. I couldn't abide her being a lesbian, as if somehow I, the model father, failed in the most essential...eventually it ruined my career. I couldn't concentrate, so I left the Pasteur Institute. They mocked me for it. Let's stop all this now. Hold this gun with a steady hand, Renée."

"Look at me, Calvin. I'm Elizabeth!"

"Yes...Elizabeth. You know what's wrong, Elizabeth? The ebullient sexual freedom France is famous for has begun to slip. People are so damned frustrated they take it out in acts of revolution."

"Are you leaving or staying?"

"Leaving—leaving on the night train to Marseilles. Julien will teach you to shoot!"

"For how long? Two months? You won't be back?"

"Yes, two months."

"I want Julien here for my French lessons."

"We've got a deal! There's my girl! Where's my unopened Scotch and the Havana cigars? Let's turn on the hi-fi! Shall we have Scarlatti?"

14

"The correspondent from *Le Monde* has called us 'un bâteau ivre', drunken ship." A student stands on stage at the Théâtre de l'Odéon, addressing the crowd of ten thousand. He wears a blue-jean jacket covered with hand-stitched peace symbols.

"Dumb imagery, fellows, for our direct democracy, don't you agree? The correspondent from *Le Monde* is the drunk one, drunk from conservative crap," another student answers him.

"Fear!" yet another one screams.

There's an air of excitement and defiance here tonight. They've been debating all day, and Colette and I are fascinated with what's going on. Scattered all over the enormous stage are frowzy ruffled skirts and blouses—costumes from another era—judges' wigs and toppled stage sets. Lying on the auditorium floor is an old chair, still sporting a sign on its back which reads, "Molière's *The Misanthrope.*" Now and then, a bold boy rushes up to the stage, places a powdered white wig on his head and delivers a pompous speech which sounds like something De Gaulle would say!

Then everyone waves their red flags (which are still being passed out at the side entrances) and roars their approval. From ornate golden balconies, activists are launching leaflets which say things like "We won't negotiate, you bastards," and "Students! Workers! Unite!"

Crumpled packages of potato chips and crusts of desecrated French bread stuffed with butter and ham are being passed from hand to hand along with cheap red wine. I want to devour the wine: its fragrance reminds me of New Orleans, my first Mardi Gras, when I wore a purple satin dress and rode an ornate purple float decorated with cerise flowers. The spectators, like these spectators, drank gallons of wine and sang to us. I can see the rats have already begun to join the students—now stunned by them, now oblivious of them. Everyone is talking to someone—that's all there is to do besides eating and cursing.

"Everything that falsifies must be discredited, boycotted, treated as contemptible.... We say all revolutionaries must now recognize it as their immediate task to denounce and deter, by any means and at any price, those who wish to falsify." A stuffy young man wearing gold-rimmed glasses talks to anyone willing to listen.

"What does this have to do with my beefsteak, buddy? You want to be in this with us, you listen to the workers!" a burly man in dirty boots answers him.

"He's listening. Don't be so rude!" a butch woman in jeans and a work shirt cuts in. "Today at Sud Aviation, we left our machines, occupied our plant, and locked up our director! We figured if the students can do it, so can we! We need a shorter work week with pay...now we'll get it!"

"Ain't she a smart girl?! Do girls join the unions at Sud Aviation? Do girls feed their families?"

"This is a rally of equally strong comrades. Girls have the same rights as..." A young Russian-looking woman in a black turtle neck sweater defends her. "When I get back to work at the T.V. station, I'm starting a feminist protest group."

"I won't take his...how dare he ask if I have a family!" The butch moves toward the worker.

"Clear off! Who are you anyway, girl? I have an urge to smack your fat ass! Down with the uppity girls! What do they know about work?"

"She's not a girl, she's a woman and I want to hear what she thinks!" I'm invigorated by the sound of my own voice.

"You American hippies!! I'm surprised you're not deafening us with your rock music. American women are all whores!!"

"Is this man a part of your revolution?" I turn to the intellectual in gold-rimmed glasses.

"Am I my brother's keeper?" he retorts.

The Russian woman holds out her hand. "Natasha's my name. Let's start the group here and now!"

"Great, Natasha. I'm Elizabeth! Where do you work?"

"The ORTF. The National T.V. offices in Paris. Here!"

"Serves all you traitors bloody right!" a balding Gaullist answers us, "Like a bunch of bitches in heat—all of you!"

"*Silence! N'interrompez pas! Un peu d'ordre! Discipline!*" The student chairman of the occupation committee screams at the crowd for order.

"You're a lot of bandits!" a laborer turns on the

student leader. "We've talked to our bosses for years, trying to make sense of this business, and you step in like a lot of ladies, tripping on your heels."

"Down with everything to do with the consumer society," another student yells. "There'll be no reason to mollify the bosses when there are no more bosses!"

"Excuse me, sir, but you students are a bunch of fascists—putting down everyone who disagrees...."

"Stop all work! We won't be stopped!" Several students shout from the stage.

The crowd starts to laugh. There's a shifting of energies as if one drama prepares the way for others. I see how dainty Colette's red bow lips look in the midst of such hatred and hilarity. Why sometimes do images begin to tremble? I watch Colette and the ruffians, and young students and workers, and girls who don't yet know they're women, standing, declaiming, crying, arguing, at the Théâtre de l'Odéon—every stair step a stage with the garnet velvet curtains and Gothic arches. The men blow their noses and pat one another's asses all the way down the aisles.

The only revolutionary thing to do is rely on our own selves, without expecting others to take care of us. Che Guevara's words come to me for some reason.

"Colette, will you move in with me, now that Calvin's gone? It'll be free rent."

"I don't know."

"Will you?"

"I can't! Jacques and I signed a lease together...."

"But I thought he pays the rent. Doesn't he?"

"Aren't you the determined one!"

"I'm lonely. Now that Calvin's gone, I don't want to be alone in the house. I've been alone so long....I've begun to think about you. Remember the woman I've told you about—Cecilia?"

"Yeah—your ex-lover?"

"I came here to forget her. She was my therapist."

"Your therapist! But I thought…"

"My therapist was my lover, Colette. Most of her therapy was phony, intellectually vague. She was always seductive, as if she had to flirt to hide her deficiencies. When she abused me, she wounded me. She recreated the terror I felt as a child. If I hired a surgeon to remove an appendix, and he left half of it, he'd be legally liable. But Cecilia runs free, blithely planning her Tuesday night consciousness-raising groups for middle-aged women, making her silly distinctions between 'aging' and 'ripening'. Frankly, I'd rather age. 'Ripening' sounds like some rank cheese or something."

❖❖❖

As Sartre himself enters the theatre to address the radicals, an enormous roar of adulation deafens the small bitter quarrels and boasting battles of the others. A silence suddenly fills the hall as he begins to speak. Tiny and ugly, the lenses of his glasses dirty from the darkening air, he says, "Violence is the one thing that remains, whatever the regime, for the students. The only relationship they can have to the university is to smash it!"

I jerk off my sweater and settle back. "Damned right, isn't he, Colette? It's impossible to escape this mob now."

"Nothing is ever impossible, my darling. Even Jacques said he would investigate that imbecile doctor of yours! Well, he didn't really want to, but I forced him to. I fought him. Come over tomorrow. Bring your overnight things. We'll be okay together, Elizabeth."

Part Six

Elizabeth

15

I'm always on the edge of things. But this time I'll complete the action. I'll have an affair with Colette, because I like her coarse hair, her lion's mane, and her blue-green hawklike eyes. Her joyfulness jogs my memory, reminding me of early morning swims in the diamond lakes of Louisiana and summer camp with tanned girlfriends.

The subway map's so clear in Paris. Only one change, at Odéon, between Montparnasse and Dausmenil, a neighborhood of small fruit stands and cheese shops. The buildings remind me of an earlier elegance, a nineteenth-century dancing elegance, now crippled by the sorrowful steps of the plumbers and watchmakers who have taken over the place.

My fears are beginning to evaporate now. Just leaving Calvin's house I feel better. I step lightly, carry a snappy black overnight case. I decide to walk through the Bois de Vincennes—clear my head first to map out what I'll say to her—hell as far as that goes, what I'll say to Jacques! I don't know anything about him. I won't consider a man, certainly not a stodgy doctor, my competitor for someone like Colette.

In the woody park called the Bois de Vincennes, children run and scream at the baby swans who cavort in the Lac Dausmenil. I've never seen *grey* swans. An old woman sitting on a park bench tells me they'll start shedding their fluffy feathers for sleek white ones come November. Where will *I* be in November? Shedding what? Feeling the shadows of golden chartreuse leaves in my hair, I move dreamily to the circular rhythms of the lake. Delicate wrens and pigeons rush to the lake's edge. There, twin boys in matching white cotton shorts and socks throw cookie crumbs to the swans.

Just then, a thin, mangy German shepherd rises out of the lake, a fish or bird or something in his jaws. Gazing more closely at him, I realize someone has placed a muzzle over his nose! He can't bite or bark, and he has to dive into the lake to drink. Every time, he takes a chance on drowning.

"Shouldn't we take off the muzzle?" I ask the woman.

"What if he's rabid?" she says.

He seems crazed from so much deprivation, running this way and that, chasing the well-trimmed poodles and black and white terriers. They, unaware of his despair, wag their tails in indiscriminate friendliness. The eyes of animals are purely soul, aren't they? I remember my black cat, with his remarkable round eyes. He slept in the small of my back as if to say, "Rest awhile, I'll be with you when you're sad."

Why can't we help this poor dog? I want to insist. But I know it's no use. We can't save everything, not the whole damned world. I turn away toward a bridge overlooking the rustling plum trees, the pregnant mothers. The lime sunlight highlights noisy Algerian children and mallard ducks who dive now into their ninety-degree-down position, feathers trembling, eating god-knows-what down below.

She'll be pleased to see me, I hope. Colette. Oh, just the sound of her name. (I'm crazy 'bout you, Colette.) Colette lives on the rue Claude Decaen, two blocks south of the large boulevard Dausmenil and parallel to it. Out of the park and into the colorfully swirling streets. No stopping except for flowers. "Who will buy my sweet red roses, two for a penny, who will buy my sweet red..." I haven't sung that for months, not since some Christmas fest. Where was it? Unexpectedly, I conjure up my comfortable old house in the Berkeley hills, friends around a jewelly Christmas tree, with the Bay Bridge visible in the distance. "Two dozen red roses," I demand of the flower keeper. He's a part of my mood, too. Only seven more blocks to her house. I could stand under her window and sing.

I don't let myself run. I enter #44 rue Claude Decaen with a wildly beating trepidation in my heart. In typical French fashion, six apartments surround a square with a concièrge's cottage at the entrance. The gate's wide open. A two-year-old—is it a boy or a girl?—a completely androgynous-looking ragamuffin nearly runs me down with a tricycle. The concièrge is screaming a string of filthy French curses at her son-in-law, who sounds as if he's been drunk all his life. I look away from them, and realize that #44 is the number for all six apartments! What did she say? Top on the right side or the left? Choosing left, I trudge up the dirty, narrow stairs and ring the bell. A middle-aged Frenchman, dressed in a red turtleneck and tight black jeans, answers the door.

"Jacques?" I inquire.

"That's right. You must be Elizabeth O'Connor, judging by your accent!"

I want to hide my luggage. I feel unbelievably awkward with him. "Is Colette at home?" I manage to smile.

"No, but come wait with me. She's out for her afternoon dance lessons. I believe it's jazz—I'm never sure! Colette's very self-centered. She'll be bloody home when she damned well feels like it. She's no more a dancer than I am! I'd like to burn all her bloody costumes!"

I'm alarmed at the chaos in this place, alarmed at his anger and at the flowers I'm holding. I would have imagined white walls and some of Manet's work. Instead, the wallpaper in the single sitting room is busy with yellow, pink, and green balloons. There's a solitary heater there, and no fan to stir the sour air. In the bedroom, a roll-away couch is still out, its sheets mashed and wound as though its occupants had been fighting, perhaps in the early morning hours. The wallpaper here is *really* vulgar: two nineteenth-century English ladies step gingerly into a rowboat paddled by a gentleman dressed in grey. This is a wall of olives and greys.

"I understand you're studying to be a doctor." I'm determined to wait for her.

"That's right. Here, give me the flowers. They're too extravagant, my dear!"

"I understand you work at the Pasteur Institute."

"That's right! I'll be the best damned internist that place has trained in ages."

"Do you know the reputation of an older internist? My *own* doctor, in fact? Calvin Douglas? He's retired—"

"Colette's been telling me about *him*!" I see something snap in Jacques as if he has summed me up and is now ready to act on it.

"Didn't Colette ask you to investigate…"

"Women always want things from me! What do *you* want? It's weird, one doctor spying on another one."

"I just want to know about his research, his contribution to the field of endocrinology."

"That's not what you want to know! Can't you be real? You're scared shitless."

16

There it is, finally. The turn of the key. I can almost feel her fingers moving through my hair.

"Well, if it isn't Ginger Rogers!" snarls Jacques.

Sighing, Colette walks away from him. "Have you treated our guest with courtesy? Have you offered her the refreshment she needs? Oh, and the flowers, Elizabeth…"

"What *does* she need? What do you want, Elizabeth?"

"I want—I need—tea! Strong, hot tea!"

Jacques goes to the kitchen. He bangs the rusty teapot on the old gas burner and comes back with an ugly brown cup, cracked and black at the base and filled with some yellow tepid tea. Colette, embarrassed, brushes her lips in a peremptory way. I've never wanted a *real* woman, one with curly blond hair and hands I can touch without guilt. I imagine picking balloons from the wallpaper, flying all the pink ones, holding on to their strings, soaring with my darling Colette into the burning coral skies. Oh, I'm so attracted! I want to cradle her head.

"What have you and Jacques been doing with yourselves?"

"We talked a little about Calvin. He didn't seem to want—"

"I'm going to help Elizabeth *this* week. I'll make time for her."

"Don't patronize her." Colette wants to embarrass him. I can tell.

"I'm not getting ready for some women's-lib shit, am I? Because this is France, not America where the men are queers and wimps."

Colette looks at her feet as if she can't stand for me to see him getting the best of her.

"Colette," Jacques continues, "I hope you're using your allowance wisely now, and have you even acknowledged Elizabeth's flowers?"

Colette looks him squarely in the eye.

"It's not an allowance. I earned it, catering to your whims. And Elizabeth knows I love her flowers. I tried to thank her when I walked in, but *you* cranked up your noisy voice!"

"Oh, Colette, let's not—" I say.

"Easy for *you* to pacify him. You don't know what I put up with. You think straight women are copouts, but *you're* naïve."

"Colette, I'm so sorry…"

Jacques moves his face very close to mine. "Don't make scurrilous implications about Elizabeth. She's as normal as we are."

"Normal's a relative concept. Wouldn't you agree, Colette?"

"I do, but Jacques doesn't. And the flowers are perfect! Almost too perfect for me."

"No, they're what you deserve!"

Jacques appears now to be agitated, to be scurrying over the floors, first eyeing Colette's red costume—the red satin bodysuit, newly glazed like the sharp glaze on baked yams, the tiny rolled silk straps hiding their hard elastic, the green and blue rolled roses right where her breasts begin, the simple silver chain. The satin seams make a V of her small waist. He closes his eyes just for a minute. Is he thinking, What would it be like to be Colette today, with this outrageously serious and sensuous brunette bringing her flowers, waiting for her, praying—yes, goddammit, praying.

"It's just been too lousy." Jacques speaks to the wall, then blinks at me and finally holds still. I can see him shift attitudes, brush the frown from his thin lips—attempt to appease Colette before he leaves for school.

"Colette, sit down. Let me make you some tea."

"Not tea. Champagne! Elizabeth and I crave champagne and clam spaghetti for our supper. That's what we yearn for, don't we?"

"Well, my old dears, who'll make your fancy supper? I have to be going. A man's job, and all that."

I'm aware once more of their dingy apartment, like grad-uate-student housing. Outside, the concièrge is trying for the tenth time to subdue her drunken son-in-law with her obscene epithets. But the child is nowhere to be seen, whisked away, so the family can continue its precious fighting, I assume. Like those scenes from my own childhood....

"Jacques, don't forget to bring back some apples for our lunches. Okay? When will you—?"

"Home by ten, right after my class." He pulls tight his faded black jacket.

"Nice of you to fix my tea, Jacques." My mind and heart are just exploding.

"See you."

He walks out.

"Everyone's crazy here. It comes with the territory. I guess you're shocked by the surroundings. Right, Elizabeth?"

"Yes...no...I know what it is to be poor, to be a student, needing just about everything...."

"Do you?"

"Oh, Colette. Move in with me! You've seen Calvin's mansion...the great bedroom overlooking the rose garden. Montparnasse, the *exciting* neighborhood."

"You know I can't, darling."

"Why?"

"Jacques would never forgive...!"

"And how important is that?"

"I can't just pitch him aside. He's been my closest friend..."

"And lover?"

"Yes, sometimes,...but it can't compare with..."

"With what, Colette?"

"Come here, Elizabeth, I want to paint you!"

"Why, for God's sake, with so little—"

"We have all the time in the world!"

"*You* do, Colette. I'm getting old."

"You're still young, you silly."

Colette sets up her easel with a playful swoop, like a gay porpoise. A thousand fuchsias flutter their purple petals over her breasts, so large for such a small girl. Has she perfumed her nipples under the red satin dance outfit? I want her breasts to smother my nose, my eyes, my mouth. Red satin and the fast lanes of New York, I think. Yes, the happiness of Broadway, the

Indian vendors' open trucks and their red string purses and the stolen watches all golden and black... Bill Blass, Pierre Cardin and the rest. Who could resist such things?

"If you paint me, you'll either capture my soul or see the wart under my right foot."

Colette mixes her oranges, yellows and tans. My complexion is colder than that, as cold as the insulting sweetness of white mothballs. Cold as my mother's bone china. Now, in the yielding light of late summer, a face begins to take shape on Colette's canvas. My face, *there* on her easel, but not quite right. Those deep-socketed eyes are more haunted than I remember, almost angry, and the nose is bigger, like an old blubbery Irish comedian. Colette shakes her right hand with its blond baby hairs, painted nails, a false pearl stuck on the ring finger. But it's the muscled thumb that makes all her artistic decisions. Probably this is all for the best. I couldn't, wouldn't know how to undress her, or what to do with those volatile lips, those valentine lips, so funny and full.

It occurs to me that memory itself is sexual, a Dionysian attachment to the past that others want to simplify, sanitize. I'll never want anyone like I wanted Cecilia. I let myself imagine her. Now I *really* need you, Cecilia. Sitting with your legs wide open...the therapy hour and you're wearing a nursing bra and nothing else. I'm fighting to pull you to my mouth, and you're sighing, relenting, opening your mouth to take in my eyes.... You encircle my sighing eyes with your tongue.

"Elizabeth, where *are* you?" says Colette.

"Here with you!"

I laugh to myself. They're nothing alike. Colette's delicate throat is like the purple throat of an iris.

Cecilia's body was oddly disproportionate, the top like the bulky mastheads on Swedish frigates. I always wanted to ask her about the scar between her collarbones, the whitish pinkish scar under the soft, inevitably aging neck. Did some insanely jealous lover try to slit her throat? Her legs were long and lightly muscled, as though one part of her body had nothing to do with the other.

Colette pours turpentine into the waiting cans, opens the window so we can breathe, thrusts her brushes into the oily liquid, then wipes them on clean cotton rags and turns them upside down.

"Jacques is uneasy about our friendship."

"I know."

To want a woman like a fix—is that the only way? Colette's easier, though. One expects less after the death of the first lover, almost as if only the astonished wound really feels betrayal. All else is numb, nonexistent.

17

The next morning, the phone rings over and over again, like a callow teenager nagging his mother. Unsure whether Calvin has left, I pick up the receiver to hear an irate voice saying, "Your old man called after you left Colette last night. He was hysterical. He kept saying, 'You have no right to interfere with the privileged relationship between doctor and patient.' So I've got something for you, missy. I could have told you when you made your queenly visit yesterday. But I didn't want Colette involved. I don't want her dragged through these dirty disclosures. What's more, Colette and I can't be carrying on with you. If you want the disgusting exposé, meet me at the Paul Verlaine Café in the Place d'Italie. One hour." Then nothing. Jacques sounds like the ruffian he is. If Julien's home, I'll take him with me; if not—Oh, God! The sitting room is appalling this morning. Calvin must have smashed the glass mirror and scattered torn photographs all over the floor last night. In one fragment, I see two childish hands holding each other. Calvin's gold ring, the one his father gave him, lies half-melted in the filthy fireplace.

❖❖❖

Jacques is smoking a cigarette when I arrive. At the desolate café, we're the only two sitting under the umbrella in the tepid sunshine. With his short hair and pig-fresh, cleanly shaven cheeks, he looks more German than French. He's breathing heavily.

"Calvin kept barking at me on the telephone, 'I would have thought an intern would be more discreet.' He thought I'd already told you. The connection was atrocious. It sounded like Spain, not France. I left my research for this soap-opera investigation into a doddering lunatic pervert!"

"*Was* he in France?"

"I can't tolerate this kind of nonsense!"

"What are you trying to say?"

"I'm asking you to stop meddling in our business once and for all, for Colette's sake."

How many times, I wonder, was Renée boxed in like this? Was her writing enough to stop the mortification? Did she wash her blouses over and over again? There's a tinny sound, as if Jacques were opening a Christmas box of newly-baked fruitcake. He slams shut the lid, inhales deeply, and holds out a newspaper article to me.

"Here. I'm giving you this. In exchange, I want you to disappear! Colette and I don't socialize with *your* type. Colette can't help you with this!"

I look away, breathe deeply, and imagine that Renée's standing here with me. Such a strong sister she is...

I see the edges of a newspaper article, the terrible look in Calvin's eyes, and Calvin so young, only forty-five, my age. I remember the ugly box of books in Renée's study. I'll have to read it now, just as if I had picked up a boring newspaper and began scanning the shenanigans of the American stock markets. What would it be like to be someone else? Just a sweet pleasant woman, who didn't read, didn't obsess, didn't judge and analyze everything and everyone? In electric shock, presumably, all the synapses shoot off, then there's the resting, the velvety darkness, the emptiness, with the clean sheets to cushion you. Was it like that for him?

"I'll take it then, Jacques."

There it is! Dated June 15, 1953—fifteen years ago. And Calvin appears to be desperate, angry. I've seen that look before, on the train from Fuveau to Paris, and again when I refused to let him in my room. Because I've always known that my knowing made me different, made me a visionary, though I've hated the burden of it. I've been so afraid of my dreams. I often see things now with my brother's eyes, as if he's invaded me, saying, "Elizabeth, your energy's enough for us both. Let me inhabit you." Last night, I dreamed he was seventeen again, the age I always make him, with me twenty-two, before my marriage began....

I pretend deafness to his curses. I fall back to sleep. All at once, I can't anchor myself to that mattress any more, though it's become truly my own. In the far corner of my bleakest pupil there is a grave, a very small mound of fresh dirt.

"Wake up, you've got to help me, my brother," I whisper softly, so he won't stare at me with his huge, angry, dilated, blue-black eyes. Sensing my anguish, he hesitates, then gets up sloppily like the adolescent slob he really was, and walks doggedly to the graveside.

"Elizabeth. *Read* the article, don't just glance at it." Jacques glares at me.

I wrap two arms round my chest, a wheezing asthmatic chest which feels like an iron lung full of bees.

"I said I'd read it."

Calvin Douglas M.D. Sentenced
to Four Years for Forcing
13-Year-Old Patient into Sodomy

I don't want him to hear me breathing.

The article seems incredibly present, and the newspaper looks like yesterday's paper.

"For forcing a thirteen-year-old patient!" So terrible to read, really. Yet once I'm finally drawn to that page, I feel like a bystander at a fatal accident who can't help staring at the bleeding man's crushed head under his motorcycle.

A columnist, a woman, writes—

"Outwardly, Calvin Douglas appeared normal. But to those who knew him intimately, he behaved like a Dr. Jekyll and Mr. Hyde. As Dr. Jekyll, he was a respected researcher at the Pasteur Institute, a man who found new methods for measuring insulin levels in diabetic children. He was gentle as a physician, an American expatriate, of good family. His father was a Supreme Court judge in Massachusetts. However, on the Mr. Hyde side, he was explosively violent when crossed, an alcoholic with a penchant for sex with girl children that went beyond his own daughter, whom he said was the center of his life.

"The solid facts of Dr. Douglas's life were detailed in a lengthy probation report filed after the ex-Institute research physician received a four-year prison sentence for the sexual molestation of Laura Delvaux, a thirteen-year-old girl from a wealthy family in Paris. Douglas could be eligible for parole in fewer than two years."

The xeroxed article goes on for three more paragraphs. I'm crying now. I lived with a man who could do these things. I trusted him. I'm so afraid, so ashamed. Was Cecilia also capable of sexual violence? And if so, is that what *we* were doing? Hating ourselves and each other? I've got to find Renée, hear her side of it, really take in the fact that she's alive, doing worthwhile work.

"Leave me alone for a few minutes, Jacques. I'll be going once I've settled my thoughts. Where'd you find this article?"

"In the Pasteur Institute Library. In the Documents Room, to be exact. It's on *loan*," Jacques enunciates his long *o*. "You remember our agreement. Leave Colette alone! I don't have the patience for any more of this crap. You pay the bill. It won't begin to cover my time."

18

On the way back to Montparnasse, I concentrate on Julien. From time to time I touch the article, which is folded over twice so it fits into my pocket. Julien has never stopped reassuring me of his trustworthiness. Once when we were together, he said, "Just know as you're walking around this great city that I'm out there somewhere watching over you." And then he said, "I want our relationship to be completely happy—that's what I want for us." The last time we talked, he gave me detailed directions to La Palette, the restaurant on rue de Seine where the Left-Bank writers and revolutionaries meet. Our dinner was troubling. Whenever I tried to focus the conversation on him, he'd hedge.

"The only thing I can tell you about my girlfriend Françoise is that I'm afraid of her. I worry I'll crush her, that she's too physically weak. It's been that way with many women."

"You sound as if you're still caught in your infant sister's web, Julien."

I want to be honest with him, but he changes the

subject. I've got to call him one day soon. Though he's probably younger than I, he makes me think of a courageous old rabbi, one who's saved countless orphans. At other times he's like Dostoevsky, reincarnated, dark and brooding, saying "Eventually, our dreams do come true, but the form they take is often unrecognizable."

I walk faster as I approach Calvin's house. There's more glass on the sitting-room floor than I remembered. It's as if this morning were years ago, as if I've been on this treadmill of unhappiness most of my life. Calvin's bedroom swirls in papers. He's thrown his ragged sweaters and trousers all over the floor. It occurs to me that this is the first time I've seen this room, though he often asked me to sit with him here by the fire. A green blanket and a hard black revolver rest precariously close to the fireplace, where an old fire still simmers with bitterness. Where is Mia, I wonder? The feeling is familiar. I'm wandering alone in an empty house, wondering if everyone else has moved away.

I go to the kitchen for some lunch after the poisonous breakfast with Jacques. The oven is still on, and the refrigerator door swings back and forth. A jar of French Poupon mustard has shattered onto the tiles, like the rich ochre Gauguin might have used so many years ago. Eggshells are still stuck to the countertops. When I find an empty bottle of Chivas Regal propped up next to the toaster, I don't even flinch. After all, Calvin drank a bottle every night!

I go back to his bedroom and throw his green blanket onto the bed. Of course, he's not there anymore. He was an odd kind of father for a few weeks. My compulsion to form families out of the unfamiliar is something I don't understand. There are no shells in the gun, it was probably just an empty gesture.

But what are these pictures, all in a neat pile on his desk? Is this some kind of joke, some ugly jest...a warning? Did Calvin place these photographs here so I would have to find them? One lies separate from the others. It's Renée in a one-piece red bathing suit, wearing heels. Maybe...fifteen! A delicate pink conch shell weights the edge of her picture. I feel sick at the sight of it. Calvin did that with such precision and then he left a note, written in a meticulous hand, in red ink:

> My dearest Renée,
>
> Please forgive me for the embarrassment I've caused you all these years! You must know by now that I was wrongly accused. That I would never accost my own patient, not to speak of a small girl. I gave that girl my best! I was able to successfully treat a severe case of infantile diabetes which had been completely overlooked by the other doctors.
>
> The child was fainting for lack of insulin. Her teachers identified her as "retarded" until I came along. Her parents were insane to make such accusations against me. Just insane! And I, even to this day, continue to live out an unjust sentence.
>
> I'm leaving tonight for Fuveau, perhaps to die there, who knows? I want a reunion before I die. Please, Renée, you have the number—77-45-48-21. Call me, Renée...if you're still alive. Let's walk the dusty lanes of Provence again. Just once, my only darling daughter. Goodbye.
>
> Your father

Why can't I judge him? I've *seen* the article. I'm glad he's in Fuveau now, as he *should* be.

Calvin didn't disinherit Renée. She abandoned him! Poor, dear Calvin, so like me. My old Calvin... both our lives ruined with obsessions...your passion for Renée...mine for Cecilia. And I let you down. But Renée is the one who deserves my compassion.

He's not in the house anymore. He's already in Fuveau, drinking in that bar. Perhaps I'll call, just to be certain he's still alive. I'll say, "Calvin, do the farmers remember our meeting in Le Club Joyeux?" He's a man who keeps his word, Calvin is. He won't come back. He's a man from an old responsible family in the East. I'll write him. That'll work. I'll say, "Have you begun your memoirs, Calvin, far from this student revolution? I can see your point of view!"

"Where are you, Mia?" I call. "Haven't you fixed my lunch?" Mia should work for *me* now. Someone's got to be here with me. "Where are you, Mia?" But she doesn't...

I'll just talk to myself, I'll just pick up the gun and talk to myself. I say to myself, "Remember Renée's notebook, the hidden story in the small, silent study? You owe it to yourself...."

I'm powerful with this gun. I can use this, Cecilia. Don't you forget it, either. I can get this thing through customs, Cecilia, you blithering bully, you goddamned butcher of a therapist. Why aren't there rules for what you did? You fucking cowardly bitch!

But it occurs to me that she suffers, too, though not the way I do. She'd always pontificate in therapy. "You want me to feel just like you do, Elizabeth. That's not the way people work!" She'd jerk her shoulders in a gesture of contempt. Do you experience the hollowness, too, Cecilia? I'd ask. And she'd look at me with a blankness, almost as if she were paralyzed from the shoulders up without knowing it.

I walk more quickly now, past the elegant dining table, past the Directoire chairs and cabinets. I stop to stare at my own bedroom. The bed is stripped of its blue satin sheets! Why? Why don't you leave me alone, Calvin? I'm not ever going to sleep here again. I have to move out of this place. I don't let myself remember my mother's opulent bedroom, her long pregnant days, the petulant whippings with stripped magnolia branches when I came home at sunset. Five years old. I'm not ever coming back, mother, so you can put down those switches and get on with your complaints. I'm not ever coming back! I need Renée now. I believe Renée's life is a lot like mine. Perhaps it wasn't just a coincidence, finding her notebook weeks ago.

❖❖❖

My nerves begin to be soothed when I enter that spotlessly clean study. It's as if some diligent mother has tried every day to wax those floors, some attentive mother who has vowed to preserve the spirit of her daughter's favorite room. The little desk is just as beautiful as I remember, cherry wood with a lovely sheen to it. And beside the desk, a Persian rug sparkles with purples, reds, and cobalt blues. A green lamp spreads its shamrock glow all over the room. I hurry to the desk hoping that Renée's notebook has not been taken away. I need to experience her presence. I want her to remind me that very intelligent women *really do* survive. There again in her hidden study, still centered, as if Calvin wanted me to know her, is her letter of love to her friend.

Renée Douglas for her friend Germaine

The handwriting is young and small, like that of a fifteen-year-old. Why would Calvin keep this? Why place this in the unmistakable center of his existence? Yet these words which create a goddess out of desire are no longer so important to me. Now I want angry words to bring about changes and new clarities. Will Renée like me this way? Hell, is Renée even alive?

I suddenly see the cardboard box I refused to open before. Ripping off the metal bracket, I slam Calvin's books onto the floor: de Sade's *Sodom and Gomorrah*, Nabokov's *Lolita*, and a long treatise on infertility in a blue faltering type. I'm about to shut the box when I see another of Renée's notebooks among Calvin's meticulous notes. In a dark black script, Renée has written:

"My father has molested me for the last five years. Next year, at the end of my *lycée*, I will leave him. When my father was finally arrested last year, I rested with some relief. I was so sorry for his patient, I knew her well. My father cared for Laura Delvaux for four years before he sodomized her. He *did genuinely* love her, perhaps more than he cared for me, because she was so ill with the diabetes which left her thin and terribly nervous. I respected my father's skill and diligence in those years. His career was at its height and he was lecturing all over Europe. Yet he drank then, just as he drinks now. And his character became harsh and violently competitive when he used alcohol. My father convinced Laura Delvaux's parents to let her begin what he called an athletic sports therapy. It was just a matter of time before that Saturday afternoon....He had been drinking Scotch and chasing it down with beer. Laura came dressed in blue jeans, and he took her to the Bois de Boulogne. Four hours later a *gendarme* came to our door. I could see the girl's body in the waiting ambulance. My family has never escaped this scandal and they never will. Humiliation and disillusionment are the continuous realities of my life."

Picking up her notebook, I place it under my right arm. I ascend the stairs, one by one. On the first step I think, Renée should be my soul sister. On the second step I think, but I don't even know her. On the third step I think, Cecilia's the only one who knows my history, my emotions, my desires. I want more than anything else to send her a Christmas card. What I'll say on the card is this: "Cecilia, I still have the same intense feelings for you. Nothing has changed. Be with me, Cecilia. I love you, Elizabeth."

I could call her! There would be nothing wrong with a call. It's 11 a.m. in Paris—2 a.m. in Berkeley. I rush to my bedroom for the address book. Odd that I've forgotten her number. Oh, and yes, the 5" x 7" card she gave me before that day. Before our termination. Every hour noted—every hour she'd be in her office. I can tell if she's there now! I remember she led consciousness-raising groups on Tuesday nights. Is she leading the group now? Oh, god, no. The group ended four hours ago. I've waited too long. But all at once I feel the old familiar pain. The electricity shooting through my arms. The throat heaving up its useless heart. The tears, the anxieties. I can't start this again. I mustn't call her, anyway. But someone must...I need someone with soft fingers...Colette wanted to take me home last night. I'll call her. That's it...the day was dripping its crystals into the lake in the Bois de Vincennes, and Colette walking by my side. To hell with Jacques's threats and Calvin's insanity. I'm too old to waste any more time on them.

19

I picture Colette starting out for my house in the late afternoon—yes, it *is* my house now, in Montparnasse—leaving the shaded streets of Dausmenil to cross the bridge toward the West Bank. She'll be very quick and tense and glittering, as if what's left of the afternoon sun has settled on her patent leather shoes and given them speed. And all along the river, great batches of early fall tourists, the ones who waited for the fares to go down, will be leaving the *bateaux mouches,* and great batches will be getting on. She'll look up at the individual roofs of Paris, seeing their myriad square chimneys, very pink and varicolored under the coral pearl sky. She'll see the mist beginning to caress that army of stones around the river, beginning to caress the beggars who walk even now through the city's contorted alleys toward the coolness of the river, who even now stake out a spot beneath the city's bridges. At some point along the way, Colette's excitement will mount—she'll become impatient and duck into the Métro, perhaps at the Odéon. Soon a man across from her will wonder why she doesn't flirt with him. Eventually he'll give up. Then, arising into the elegant gaiety of Montparnasse, she'll find my front door. At the sound of Colette's feet on the great granite step, I will have finally achieved a kind of balancing of new desire with old despair.

I wait at my darkening window with a letter in my hand. When Colette actually does step up to the door, she hesitates and finally knocks. I'm afraid even to leave my bedroom but I force myself down the stairs.

"*Ah, ma chérie! Tu es revenue!* You have come back at last—and Calvin's gone away! *Salut!*"

"*Salut,* Elizabeth. *Je suis ravie!*"

"Would you like a drink? Champagne?"

"And clam spaghetti too?"

We chuckle. She accepts my goblet, playing with the crystal mist on the foamy head of the Dom Pérignon champagne.

"He didn't know what to do with my request, did he?"

"What request?"

"For champagne and clam spaghetti. For us."

"No, he didn't! Excused himself with the demands of a man's work, a man's calling, if you will."

"I'd like to tie him to a chair and make him watch us tonight. Do you have a calling, Elizabeth?"

"Yeah, it goes, 'Let the flower of your life's force bloom'...a Buddhist truth, I think...and it closes with, 'Even if it's of no avail.'" I'm laughing at the image of fat Jacques, tied to a chair.

"Is your life force flowering?"

Colette's too literal much of the time. But *I* can hardly discipline my hands. They want to slide up and down her legs, rub her pubic hair, put their middle fingers in the middle and rub her until she cries for my tongue. "Put it all the way up," she'll say. "Harder, Elizabeth." She'll put her cunt on my face, straddle my lips and rock herself, ride me like the thoroughbred she really is.

"Elizabeth, do you hear me? How is your life force flowering?"

"Well—I came here to write. That's the shape of my flower—a novel, I think, about women and their obsessions. It may have a happy ending now. Who knows!"

"How much have you written?"

"You've *seen*, Colette. Not much! But I've started to read again, anyway."

"I'm not criticizing you. Some people would never have escaped Calvin."

"Yes, I know...I'm beginning to recognize what's wrong with Calvin. What I don't know is why *I* was complicitous."

"Elizabeth, can we dance, here in this fancy room? I feel closer to you now."

"I think I can arrange that!" I pour out two more glasses of champagne and pull at her curly hair.

"We'll pretend we're Scarlett and Rhett. I need a little rest from your seriousness!"

"If we're doing that, why not Scarlett and Melanie?"

"But who'd be Melanie?"

We chuckle and jostle our arms, our legs touching, moving them in—moving them out, dancing.

She takes my hand and lightly kisses the tips of my fingers. "We'll be the best of friends." She laughs.

Somehow this house has become a house of women tonight. I find myself wishing Renée were here, too, to calm me and reclaim her own place.

"Are we dancing together tonight to celebrate Calvin's leaving?"

"Why not? No law against dancing. Dancing is what *I* do for a living, when Jacques is being stingy!"

"Where do you dance?"

"I'd rather not—not tonight—"

I can sense the danger in her eyes. She lowers them for a long minute, and when she looks up, they're a shade lighter than before.

"My roots keep showing, that's all, Elizabeth."

"Colette, my family wasn't poor, but they were so disturbed that I've carried their despair with me all over the place, even to Paris. Yet we *can* make better dreams, we've *both* lived in such tight places."

Colette seems happier now, relieved.

"I'll find us some music!"

It won't hurt to try, anyway. I've waited for weeks. Oh, God, I *want* this to happen.

"Come here, Elizabeth." She holds out a new shining, silver goblet full of champagne.

We toast. Her mouth puts a deep pink lipstick print on the rim. She plays Janis Joplin on the hi-fi. We're moving with our legs jammed together. She's a good dancer. Supple, yet knows the right steps. She guides me, this Colette, this little child dancer, this erotic child-woman I want so badly. Colette's always cool when you get right down to it, I think, and I'm always hot.

Now she's doing it. I can feel her middle finger in my ear—pushing up and down.

"I want you," I say.

"I want you, too." And she touches my cheek with her tongue.

When the music stops, we stop too.

"Let's play the same record again."

I agree with her. I don't want to think, or try too hard. Once again we hear that violent voice of another sad girl of the southern American cities, Janis Joplin.

This time I put one arm around her waist and another around her shoulders.

I can tell she's shivering, almost convulsive.

"Colette, let's get into bed. We'll rest together. It'll be fine."

"You won't push me, will you?"

"I care about you, Colette. This isn't a seduction, for god's sake!"

We walk up the stairs again, this time holding hands. Suddenly my foot catches on the stair, I'm falling, about to fall on my chest when Colette catches me, wipes away a tear, and straightens my hair. I mustn't be so sad now. I mustn't dream of Cecilia. Not for me the deep plunge of the soft belly, my mouth inert from such dumb desiring. Cecilia, Cecilia, my rapture for you has blinded me to everyone else. Maybe there's something beyond this, though, something more real than my enrapturing of your body.

Yet it's true that I told Cecilia—it seems light years away now—I said, "You quit your job, and I'll quit mine. There'll be nothing shameful about our passion then. We'll join the Peace Corps, maybe, and live in India or Ceylon. We'll say we're sisters because we really are, my beautiful therapist." And Cecilia smiled when I said that. There were never any interventions then, no questions about the miniatures or the classical music I brought to her. I find myself even today looking through the Parisian quays for little cars to send her, little miniature sports cars, something, anything to evoke a possibility, our living museum of fantastic hopes. Once I gave her an English taxi, a black one I bought in Bloomsbury, shiny, with intricate lettering on its doors. She held it a long time, turned it over in her hands, turned her Marilyn Monroe heart-shaped face to mine and said, "Shall we pretend to be riding in this?" I answered her, "Yes—tell the driver to drive us all the way to Cornwall where we'll take a bed and breakfast in Penzance." And then I started to walk out of her office! "Virginia Woolf lived every summer near Penzance," I said, and Cecilia, flirt that she always was, threw me a kiss as I descended the stairs, back to something I called reality, real only because I people it with her hands, her hair, our kissing, our living for days, for the rest of our lives in fact, in a cottage, someplace where fuchsias bloom near the doorways and white horses run in the goldenrod fields, and two tabby cats tumble and beg us to feed them as we treat ourselves to strawberries and white wine.

"Elizabeth, are we walking up to your room?"

I'm amazed to hear Colette again, so near me. I've got to keep Colette so Cecilia goes away to another place. Hell, she's probably already in another place and already done it again to another client, charming her, fixing their therapy in an inevitably frozen erotic arc.

"What will I do, I wonder?"

"What? Elizabeth? Will *we* do? Go to your room or another?"

"The room with the Rossettis, the room Renée's mother...okay?"

"Sure. I like those purples and blues...I like you, Elizabeth."

Suddenly I'm embarrassed to love this woman in

the same place as the same man I...That's okay, I say to myself. Wouldn't Cecilia also be shy if *we* were here in this odd circumstance, this house belonging to someone called Calvin Douglas, my sadistically tender man, my old doctor.

"Colette, this may not be the right time, you know?" I see the relaxation around her mouth, the little pouting smile.

"What about just spooning—me on the inside, you on the out?"

"Yes...the deep sleep of the paired, I want *that* tonight, too."

"And then there'd be no lies for me to tell Jacques, either!"

"So has Jacques won this battle, Colette?"

"Do you have to bring him into this?"

"He's here, anyway."

"Jacques supports me, that's all."

"He seems edgy, almost violent sometimes. Does he..."

"I'm used to him, Elizabeth. I don't want to come home to an empty house."

20

Descending into the morning's vacuousness, back out to the hotly disappointing streets of the Parisian summer, Colette moves to a slower tune, a more thoughtful design, and the close dancing we did in the night is dead. She walks, however, with determination when she sees the Métro. I know. From my window, I watch her depart, take the early morning train to Dausmenil, to her dirty raucous flat, to her keeper, her violent lover, her man of medicine...her ochre paints and pink balloon wallpaper all just waiting for Jacques. And what a sham *he* is! But then I can't possibly judge the imprisoning powers of the sado-masochistic passions. For of course de Sade is the patron saint of all Catholic countries. And Cecilia would fit in fine here with me in Paris. We would continue our chess game with its vicious pawns desiring each other, lying in wait for each other, hating each....All of us would have been happier if Cecilia had just stayed in her hick hometown in southern Florida. I can just see her there with her dumb husband raising scrawny kids and vine tomatoes. But I'll think now of Colette's underground journey home to Dausmenil. Is she mentally marking her defenses, mending her image as the poor honest artist with her incredible talent and sad family to feed? That family made up of her weary mother and absent father, the American family which is all too familiar now? "To become a great painter, you have to take a vow of poverty, but I've already done that!" I remember how she'd say these outrageous things to the male students at the École des Beaux Arts—with her sharp cynicisms and flauntingly frank blue-green eyes. But her funny aphorisms were also excuses to accept Jacques's money, and her deeply felt desire for Jacques, with his pull toward brutality, is too crazy. Sometimes I see her bruises under her long-sleeved black nylon blouses, and once when we were crouched on the boulevard St.-Michel with burning cars all around, she turned to me deadpan, almost as if she were addressing someone else, "You'd never hit me, would you, Elizabeth?" I knew then that I wanted her. But that was then. Now the student revolution has failed. De Gaulle let them raise hell until the bourgeoisie grew weary of the rats in their streets amid their weeks-old garbage, and their patisseries no longer produced the *petit déjeuners*. The television sets never showed a damned thing to soften the devilishly inconvenient chaos for those critically stubborn and penurious people, the French middle classes who stomach de Sade as long as he remains safely stuck in his political prison. And I, too, am stuck in the middle. I, too, feel the weariness, long for the comforts of food and T.V.

But I must turn to claim my own present. I must find Renée. That's my project now. It keeps me awake. I'm aware, somehow, that she's my other side, maybe my shadow. More likely, though, she's my light. I'm sick from this absence of women. Yet I have an intuition about our meeting, that it will be like a ripple in a field of daffodils. The yellow silken flowers will become the tousled curls of young women, waiting for me at home with a sweeter affection than anything I've ever known before.

Julien will help me find her. I've got to call him. His brother-liness is an ever-present intelligence, an ever-present comfort. I've worried about Julien's alienation from Françoise. He's been so unhappy about his girlfriend.

"Julien, can you come for supper tonight?"

"Ahh—I've needed to talk to you. I've been concerned."

"How about seven, then?"

When Julien knocks on Calvin's great medieval door with its iron-like armory, I feel the windows flutter with fresh air.

"I've brought you these purple cyclamens. They'll bring you good luck!"

Julien takes a big spoonful of the *boeuf en daube* I cooked this morning and let simmer in its rich winey sauce all afternoon. He places it neatly on his plate between two slices of French bread. He opens his bottle of red wine, a Mouton-Cadet from Bordeaux. And we toast to our deepening friendship.

"I just want to stop loving my own damned loneliness so much."

"I know. That's how we're alike. Whenever Françoise disappears or acts distant with me, I fall back into my seclusion. It becomes my exactitude against her unpredictability."

But with Richie Havens on the turntable and

cognac in our coffee after dinner, nothing can be too sad tonight. I want to obliterate *all* my fears. Perhaps I can just *like* him, just rest easily with him, without the insufferable dramas of suffering and release, suffering and sex, suffering and suicide. Because I trust his deep sweetness.

"You *do* seem like a different woman tonight, Elizabeth, different from the one I knew even a few weeks ago. You seem more resilient."

"Maybe I'm *acting* differently. It's a start, anyway. One time you told me that Calvin's daughter was like me. How ?"

"The physical resemblance. The two of you are hauntingly similar. Especially your eyes and Renée's eyes—there's a freedom there."

"Is Renée with someone now?"

"I don't know. Calvin has shown me photographs of Renée and her female lovers."

"But didn't he disapprove?"

"Just a cover-up, Elizabeth, for something more immediate, some family secret I can't unearth."

"I saw the newspaper clipping. I know about it."

"Newspaper clipping?"

"It was so dreadful."

"I entreat you, Elizabeth."

"Remember I told you about Colette's roommate—I may as well say it, he was her lover—Jacques."

"Of course. He was investigating something for you."

"He's at the Pasteur Institute—like Calvin was. He knew Calvin had been fired. He found the newspaper article describing Calvin's arrest. He showed it to me to shame me, and to keep me away from Colette. He wanted to make me feel unworthy of her. Like those rightists who hate anyone who think for themselves, he wanted to silence me—separate me from myself."

I hand Julien the xeroxed article.

He looks down at his feet. I see his eyelids flutter. He steadies himself, holds the chair. He reads the article and, to my surprise, sits down, and starts to cry. The first time a man ever...my brother held back his tears of disappointment for *his* father, *my* handsome father, the father who rose up each morning singing "I Wonder Who's Kissing Her Now," making pots of morning coffee and crisp bacon to obliterate his night's drinking. Julien *could* have been my brother, reborn, but he's not. Which doesn't shatter the truth of reincarnation, that we're all a part of the flower and the flower's connected to the earth and there are millions of microorganisms in the earth which breathe more deeply than I or Julien or even my brother breathed. For some reason, my brother left me and all the sweet birds in the trees. For some reason, he couldn't hear our voices. It probably had nothing to do with my irresponsibility or my father's alcoholism. Mother once had a dream in which he came home and said, "I'm sorry, it was just an accident. I didn't think of the rest of you." And he didn't—he didn't remember me, but Julien does, Julien's alive, not a part of my family, not my own blood, but someone newer and kinder....

"It's tragic that Renée had to leave home, that she's never had parents. I also want to find her and bring her back."

"And it's tragic that I lived with Calvin, trusted him, even felt an odd friendship for him."

"Isn't it natural to love the person who wants to care for you, even if he's dishonest? I still don't completely trust Françoise, but I want to believe she's loyal to me. And I think finding Renée—if we can do that—points you toward *your* future, your writing, your love for other women. I also want to find her and bring her back. I'm here to help you. Whenever you want, we'll turn this house upside down. I daresay she won't be your twin, but she'll be somebody good...."

I want to kiss Julien, but instead I just stare at him.

"And will you speak to Mia? Ask her for Renée's address? Calvin kept talking about Renée's radical T.V. station. Maybe she was a reporter for the revolution. If Mia can't help, we'll start by calling the T.V. stations."

"Mia might be too obstinate to cooperate with us. She's loyal to him."

"Yeah, but it's a beginning."

21

"You think I'm so dumb all I care about is rhinestones and black lace!" I jump at Mia's outraged response to Julien's questions.

"Get it, Mr. Julien? Mr. Jewish intellectual? I'll have you know I'm smart! And that old man paid for my spaghetti. I'm not spilling the beans on him for *you!*"

The three of us stand poised, fingering the morning croissants.

"Mia, Elizabeth also wants to find Renée. Wouldn't it be *smart* to tell us? It could be unethical to keep a daughter from her home."

"Elizabeth's a crazy patient and your head's mostly in the clouds. Even if I had a mind to, I don't know any more where Dr. Douglas put his address book."

"Didn't she work at a T.V. station?" I move to the back of the kitchen, where she's begun making café au lait. Smells like coffee from Peet's in San Francisco, ages ago.

"Dr. Douglas never *said*, at least not to me. I expect him back anyway. Any day. Ask him yourself! You two *bore* me. And Renée knows the damn way home, Julien. If she takes a mind to it, she'll be here. What a mess *that* would be."

"Calvin promised he'd stay away for two months. Is he really coming back, Mia?"

"How should I know?"

"We need to find Renée. Is it worth fifty francs to tell?"

So unlike Julien, I think, to try bribery. When Mia laughs, I know we've lost.

"Julien, you old thief, you! And *you*—an employee of the old man, you, a man of *honor!*

"Forget about us, Mia. Imagine yourself the daughter who had to leave home, frightened—"

"Cut it, Julien, and get the hell out of my kitchen!"

Julien turns his head away, avoiding her brown eyes. He takes my hand. We walk slowly toward the ornate front door, push it open, and go out into the September sun.

"I'll try again tomorrow. I have a lesson to give now. I'll call her and then you tomorrow. You know, there's a Greek restaurant I've heard about where student revolutionaries gather. It's called Ouzorie. The man who runs it is named Arestides. Why don't you find him? Ask him about radical T.V. stations."

Get right up against what you don't know and stay there, I tell myself. Even though I don't know where, if it will lead me anywhere, I've got to find that T.V. station, and I've got to find Renée. I need to recognize something in her and maybe see Colette again.

I take the underground to rue Picpus. Everything is redolent with green there, where the irises and cyclamen ignite the paths with blue and fuchsia petals, asking to be touched. I cross myself in awe of them, an old habit of magic. I never flew anywhere without doing that twice on the take-off and then holding Cecilia's picture in my left hand and my brother's in my right—my two loves. When I hear the male analysts saying things like, "Obsessions emerge from the poverties of our life experiences," I want to shout, "Bullshit, buster." Women make art out of the poverties the world shoves at them, but that art is better than goddamned suicide. And I won't commit suicide. I will act—find Renée—and together, maybe, we'll write, join a rap group, dance!

❖❖❖

It's noon when I walk into the Ouzorie. Someone who appears to be the owner peers over my shoulder as I scan the menu.

"If you've ever eaten a better Greek meal, give you back your money!" he brags.

His words are lilting, almost as if he's Irish, not Greek. I see him tap his leather sandals as though he understands what it means to be always dancing, even if I don't.

"My ex-husband, Paul, fixed fabulous Greek food, so-o-o we'll see!" I say, half wanting his big hulk of an ass to continue that dance, to invite me to dance—

"My name's Arestides. Tell the waiter I'll be watching him to see you get what you want. If you don't know *what* you want, motion me over—uh—is it Sophia?"

"No, Elizabeth!" I laugh.

"Ah, very good! An English lady, no doubt!"

"No, an American *woman*, Mr. Arestides."

"Arestides is my first name...my *only* one. Charms the ladies. Means business to the creditors!"

As I walk into the loud, pulsating dining room, I notice a small French boy wearing literally hundreds of political buttons on his jeans jacket. He's gesturing with one hand, while the other pushes a button into the face of an old man who looks like he might be Bulgarian. The man keeps repeating, "All the wealth should be divided evenly. That's what Marx wrote. That's the main thing!"

The boy's hands are nearly hitting the old man's face when he says, "The French Communists are as dishonest as De Gaulle is. They finked on us. They betrayed the cause just like he did. And the stinking bourgeoisie who couldn't take more than a few days without T.V. don't *mean* to *give* the students one franc, not to speak of dividing—"

All of a sudden, a rough, square, hairy hand comes down on the boy's shoulder.

"Learn some goddamned manners or get out of here, boy. This man's our friend."

Arestides is no one to cross! The students who sit by the boy chime in, "Yeah, man, keep it cool, will you? The man's okay."

Julien was right! Arestides' restaurant really *is* a haven for student revolutionaries. God knows what they'll do with their disappointments. God knows what I'll do with mine. I sit down in a state of camaraderie. At last, some action—some people who eat, fight, and fuck one another. I don't know why I'm at home only among beggars, revolutionaries, and lunatics. I guess they put into the world what I always hide.

"Dalmas, please, and some ouzo for starters, then a half carafe of retsina, and I'll go from there!"

"He's a character, isn't he?" The waiter is young and enthusiastic about Arestides. One imagines Arestides surrounds himself with groupies.

"Yes, I like the owner. Arestides is a riot!"

No sooner said than I see him heading for my table.

"Decided yet?" he asks.

"Just the starters," I reply.

"Will you let me order?"

"What's good?"

"Try the vegetarian moussaka. What I do is *suggest* Greek without being quintessentially Greek. Who needs the pork in the moussaka? Too rich! Right?"

"Right. What else?"

"See the shrimps on the menu? Shrimp braised in yogurt with dill seeds, and tiny stalks of shallots, all swimming in a white counterpane of cream. And with golden pools of butter to finish it off."

"My ex-husband would cook something in a green pepper-shell with rice for our colleagues on Friday nights."

"Ah, darling, you're yearning for *country* Greek food—not the Athens fancy, but food we could find on a farm. This one's on me," Arestides shouts to his adoring waiter.

"Don't *forget* that, waiter!" I yell.

"Tell me about yourself, Elizabeth, and Simon, you get me some strong coffee." Arestides jerks his thumb toward the waiter. "He's really Irish. *Simon*, you know, like 'Simon Moonan'? You like Greek coffee, Elizabeth?"

"Yeah, I do. I teach *Portrait of the Artist* in my experimental fiction class…"

"God—really? I write poetry in my spare time!"

"I do, too!" I'm ecstatically happy now. I don't give a damn if this man is lying or not. I just love his energy, the energy that Paul had—that no one since then—but I want to savor it, live in the present. "I write and I've even published some poetry—in little journals."

"Great! My ex-wife teaches here at the Sorbonne, she's an art historian, Turner, romantic stuff! Had to give up all that when I left her. You know, I've opened ten restaurants in the last twelve years!"

"A lot—Arestides! Where?"

"One's in San Francisco. Zola's."

"I'm going back there soon, you know, to Berkeley. Home. I just have to find someone first, then do some things…"

"Go to Zola's when you're home and tell my baby brother. He's there with the rest of 'em—"

"Rest of whom?"

"The gay people. God knows I don't judge 'em—just couldn't give up women."

"I feel the same way!"

"What?"

"I can't give up women either, troubling as they are."

He stops his constant foot tapping and stares at me. "Well, it's *my* loss—not yours, my friend."

We both laugh and he gulps down the nastiest, brownest cup of coffee I've ever seen.

"Where else?" I'm planning to visit every damned one of his restaurants.

"There's Emilie's and Sophia's in Vancouver and Mary's in Seattle. Enough of that. I consult to make money. Businesses drag, you know. I tell 'em *what* to advertise, how to pick the right merchandise for the right crowd. You know, I'm old enough to be your uncle!"

He's started to look around. An overweight brunette with a grosgrain ribbon running through her French braids has beckoned, and he's getting nervous. I can see his foot tapping all the harder now.

"If you, Arestides, were looking for a friend who probably worked for a radical T.V. station, where would you begin?"

"That's easy. The ORTF, the National French Television. They struck during the revolution. They were the only really cool media people!"

When the bill arrives, I see that *nothing* has been free—that I've only just enough to pay. But who would fight with such a guy anyway?

22

When I walk into the main office at the ORTF, there's a hum, a rustling of yellow papers, the fierce paragraphs, and French coffee. Typists everywhere are beating out their best stories. Small, shiny mahogany desks push up close to a central hall. Here, then, is the French television station which stood by the tough boys who never succumbed to the cops.

Somewhere back there, Renée may be writing a brilliant script for the afternoon broadcast! What a pistol she'll be when I find her. I wouldn't be surprised to learn she spearheaded the demands the ORTF made to De Gaulle. It seems only yesterday that the general assembly of ORTF asked for a forty-hour week, a lower retirement age, a national minimum wage of 1,000 francs and the creation of standing reform committees. I'm going to like Renée. I remember, too, reading Ernest Mandel's descriptions of working-class militancy, which he said transcended the material demands the unions made when they negotiated with their bosses in old and ineffectual ways. For Mandel, the most eloquent case of all was silence itself, like the silence at the Atlantic Yards at St.- Nazaire, when workers occupied the plant for ten days while ferociously resisting the union's pressure to draw up a list of demands. The staunch silences of the oppressed, husbanding their energies like a coiled spring, ready to attack.

Walking down the immaculate, narrow hall, I stop to talk to a young reporter. He's hardly older than my best graduate student at Berkeley. He seems quiet and responsible. Perhaps he's the solid base of research among all the other fiery journalists. Further down, people are eating their lunches of French bread and pâté, reading *Le Monde* and thinking of their lovers. But *there,* at the center of the inner office, I'm amazed to encounter again the woman I met at the Théâtre de l'Odeon that fateful night, May 20, when so many volatile speeches somehow freed me to tell Colette about Cecilia, about my anger, my dependency.

"Didn't you tell me then you were American?" Her English is perfect.

"Yes, and I remember you. You asked me if American women smoked opium or marijuana and were they hippies along with the guys. You're Natasha?"

"Yes, aren't you Elizabeth? You told me, 'Only the bravest women go with the hippies.' You mentioned Janis Joplin...I bought her album in a music store close to the Notre Dame the other day."

"Did you start that feminist protest group, Natasha, the one you talked about so much?"

"Oh, no—never the time. You know how it is. What are *you* doing here?"

"I'm looking for someone named Renée Douglas. She's a relative of mine!"

I feel disappointed in Natasha. I wonder what makes the difference between those who act on their dreams and those who forget them. She stares at her red painted nail and pushes back her long black hair —a measure of restraint, I guess, against her real Russian intensity. Her ancestors were poor, she had said, and I had laughed about my Irish heritage with all its Bacchic singers. She never guessed the rest— the father—the family.

"Renée Douglas *does* work here, but she's left for a short trip to Aix."

Suddenly my heart stops. I have to steady my head. "Do you know if she's seeing her father?"

"She said her father was dead."

And from the back of my brain, an image flashes...of a drunk man, going into his daughter's bedroom.

"Yes, well—I'll go. We'll see each other again soon, I'm sure. I'll be back! But can I use your telephone before—?"

"Sure." She hands me the phone, and walks back to talk to a man who tells her how great she's looking.

"Hello, Mia! It's Elizabeth. Has Renée been to our house today? Has Calvin?" I'm whispering into the receiver.

"Mama mia, you really have flipped out. No, Renée hasn't been here for twenty years. Calvin's gone south, for how long is anybody's guess. You know that!"

"But has she *called* you, Mia? Has Renée called?"
"You're *both* crazy—you and Renée both!"
"Why?"

"Hell hell hell! I have to go through this again? Yes! Renée's made my life a loony bin the last two weeks. She calls to ask about Calvin. She's heard that a *woman* is living at our house, god forbid. When I told her Calvin had gone to Fuveau, she said she'd follow him, no matter what—that she was afraid for you. Was afraid he'd take you where no one could find you. I had to give her your name so she'd let me alone!"

I remember the Mexican *ex votos* I saw in Mexico City one summer. Those religious paintings were done by anonymous painters who donated them to churches as offerings to the Virgin in acknowledgement of her divine intervention in times of severe trouble. Some part of my writing will be like that— poems of thankfulness—if I can find Renée.

Part Seven

The Return

23

The Gare de Lyon is full of students this afternoon. I wonder if these are the disillusioned students who plan to take out their spite by demonstrating and doing street theater in Bordeaux? It seems like only yesterday I got off the train here, crazy, with Calvin, not knowing why I couldn't think. But it's been four months.

The train's sides are heaving hard as it pulls into berth number 18. The breezes are already cold in the Parisian corridors of pain. I long for the heat of the south. Is Renée already there? Has she seen him or is she hiding, biding her time? Little groves of silvery green olive trees fly past me.

This afternoon, the giant daisies look blank as they move past the window. Who stripped them of their color? I've no way to buy a toothbrush. The white houses with their coral roofs are faded grey, so that one wants to wear a red silk sari to defy all this greying. I must figure out what to do about Calvin—even more crucial, about Renée. I've got to keep her alive. I need her for something important.

The mystery I'm reading is called *The Horses of Camargue.* I haven't thought about Cecilia's symbolic gift for a long time, the red rocking horse she gave me in a moment of imagined generosity. What an imbecile she is! Dishonest and dumb! Little did she know that the red rocking horse would be used to escape her phoniness, her incompetence.

❖❖❖

In Aix, the ticket taker refuses to find me a taxi. He yawns. "Can't be done, lady, it's too late." Walking in wearily to the medieval section of Aix, I see an old clock. It's three. Smoky clouds create a pall over the horizon. Was there a fire? There's a smell of ash in the air, and someone's scorched shoes are in the street. Were there men running around here with their water hoses? I concentrate hard. I need to find a room, in this section of town. I'm told the hotels are the nicest here. Across from the three-star l'Hôtel de France, a small grimy hotel still burns its single downstairs light. Take this or nothing. l'Hôtel Récamier, it's called.

"I need a room for the night," I say in my best French, knowing it's too stilted. "I've just come from Marseille. I took the last coach. I'm exhausted."

"We have only one left, Mademoiselle, with a single bed and a small sink for washing. There was a fire, and many farmers have left their houses to come here. They told me they almost suffocated when ashes flew through their windows and into their rooms."

"Where was it?"

"Southeast. Some say it was near Fuveau."

"Is there a phone in the room?"

"No, but you can use the public phone."

Looking down the hall, I see roaches crawling out of the blue carpet. I shudder, feeling a sickening déjà vu. The dingy carpet is like the one in that first hotel room in Fuveau, with Calvin, that first night when I looked hard at his dirty wet boots and then down at the carpet again. Instinctively I glance at the hotel clerk's shoes—they're dry! Dust particles have settled on every piece of furniture. The lobby's brown tables are covered with old comic books and leftover breakfasts. Someone left behind his torn sweater, with a little hole near the breast pocket. So it seems that everything makes me think of him. I've been a fool. I should have rented a car. I would be there by now.... What if she's dead? What if I've lost her, like so many others? The clerk seems to pity me.

"Just give me the number. I'll dial it," he says.

"*D'accord. C'est Paris 45-42-80-60.*"

He stares at me all the while. My jacket feels small and cold.

Julien sounds cross when he answers, and I don't blame him.

"Julien, I'm sorry, but I need to talk—"

"Where are you?"

"Aix. I got here too late for a taxi to Fuveau."

"What's happened?"

"When I walked in, there had been a fire nearby, and only one room was left. I'm afraid for Renée, Julien. What if Calvin's killed her?"

"Which hotel, Elizabeth?"

"Hotel Récamier!"

"Don't leave the hotel. You're too upset to do this alone. I'll catch the fast train. I'll be there in fifteen hours!"

"Julien—okay—I'll wait."

But once in a while, we do things instinctively. We've always been women going down a road we didn't choose and can't define for a long, long time. Then, all of a sudden, the sadness, the fears, the regrets go away and a deep blood decision has been made to move in a certain direction. *We* didn't decide it, but neither did our friends or enemies.

"Wake me at 7 a.m.," I say to the manager.

"*Oui, Mademoiselle*," he replies.

24

Between the tall hedges I see a reddish yellow glow off the cut pastures. Much of the foliage on the village periphery has been scorched. From the morning look of the dusty olive trees and the orange rocks, I know I'm back in Fuveau. But, its usual golden light has become hazy from what appears to have been a fire.

"Excuse me, Madame," I inquire. "Was there a fire last night?"

She carries a dishpan of wet laundry on her hip.

"Yes," she replies. "No one knows why."

"Where did it happen?"

"Some say near the graveyard, late last night!"

"Where's the post office?" I ask, as if seeing the graveyard again, behind me.

"There," she shifts the load on her hips and points. "I'll leave you here. I'm headed for the river to rinse my laundry."

I hand her ten francs, walk into the stone post office with its tattered notices of horsey events from other summers.

"Can you help me?" The man behind the counter looks tired.

"Maybe," he replies.

"I'm looking for Calvin Douglas. He's my American uncle. He stays here—practices—during the summers."

He scrutinizes my empty ring finger. "I know him. Gotten sullen and queer in his old age, like he can't hear anyone."

"Just his address—that's all I'm asking of you."

"Why?" He's balking.

"I've traveled a long way to find him. It's an urgent family matter."

"His daughter's here..." he says, frowning. "She looks like you!"

"Where is she? Where is Renée?"

"Just over there," he says, pointing to the old hotel.

"Thank you!" I stand still for a minute out of sheer dizziness.

When I see the old hotel again, I recognize its owner's futile attempts to modernize it. A chartreuse sign blocks the entry and is continuously flickering l'Hôtel Joyeux—Provence—Vacance. I guess *everything* in town is named "joyful". How ironic. Inside, the carpet is still a faded blue. Only two other changes are apparent. A cigarette machine, which would look better in a southside Chicago bar than here, blocks my path to the hotel keeper, and over to the right, set ostentatiously beside two overstuffed chairs, is a bright, black-veneer Chinese coffee table decorated with some purple bric-a-brac swordsmen fighting each other in the center.

"Which room belongs to Renée Douglas?"

The hotel manager is napping. He rouses himself. "Room 228. She's been out all night."

For some reason I want to see her clothes.

"I'm her American cousin. I've travelled so far to find her. There's a crisis in our family. Can I run up—to see if she's maybe come back?"

"Got some ID?"

"Yeah." I pause for a minute. "Here's my driver's license."

"Return the key before you leave."

The stairs are dark, so I prefer the wooden elevator, despite its rickety frame. A bus boy takes me up. We glance distrustfully at one another when I jerk open the accordion wrought-iron door at the landing. Someone in room 226 is coughing. Why should *Renée* put up with this sordid place? Why did she come *here?* What can come of confronting a crazy drunk?

Is that why I need her? To show me how to attack Cecilia, to attack Calvin, even when the battle is futile? Nonetheless, *how* to fight against the outrageously unjust sexual attacks, with their subtle psychological violences. Opening the door, I'm struck by her orderliness. Even this terrible place is cleared of its cobwebs when she enters it.

Her mother's photograph sits on a second-hand chest. The picture's even more charming than the one Calvin carries around. Her eyes are laughing at all fictions of logic, and her hands are animated with a dexterity as they pat her hair with impish affection. Yielding to my temptation to inspect the closet, I realize that Renée would be the sister I'd want if I had a sister. Inside, she's hung three lightly starched white blouses, two pairs of new blue jeans, and three straight skirts. Her shoes are the finest black leather, polished like a young boy's Sunday shoes. At the far end of the closet she's placed her soft leather luggage. What if she walked in? She'd wonder *who* that crazy girl could be—or would she? Has she been waiting for my tap on her shoulder, a kiss of recognition, a fulfillment? In my sophomore year at college, there was a legendary service organization called Orange Jackets. When the time came during the appointed evening in March, an older member would tap the chosen girls, and then there would be an initiation. I was one of them, so many years ago. And lately, I feel chosen again.

Outside the dusty hotel window, the corona of the morning sun makes Renée's room as hot as clothpockets. I remember shaded lights and regular breathing, Jessica's breathing, so many years ago. Suddenly I feel old. I don't want to lose her, too, I think. I envision the terrible Fuveau graveyard, I sense that the two of them are there, Calvin and Renée, in some deadly battle of wits. The graveyard—of course! Rushing out the hotel door and down the steps, I grasp the key in my pocket. I need it more than the manager does. I remember the location of the plot where Renée's mother is buried. I have a hunch that Calvin's house will be nearby. And if I can spot his silver Citroën—surely in all of Fuveau, there's only one silver Citroën—then I'll have found them!

The village square is covered in gravel, which hurts my feet. But I rush to the edge of town, and I remember the fainting old women from before, behind their black wrought-iron gates that awful night in May when I hallucinated their asphyxiation and imagined them smothered by ether, the cloths held hard over their noses by angry husbands. This time, I realize they're very much alive, even smiling at me, as suppertime draws near and they prepare their meals of Provençal chicken and saffron rice. Perhaps tonight is the celebration of a young woman's birthday, attended by her neighbors—most of whom have outlived their husbands.

As the houses become larger and the flowerbeds more sculptured, I can tell I'm close. Sensations of dismay pull at me when I see patches of burned myrtle trees and old olive groves stripped of their color. The fire must have started in the graveyard. Up the dead center of the cemetery, I can see that even the recently strewn irises have turned to ashen black. Miraculously, Renée's mother's grave hasn't been touched. Instead, the moon-white sycamore which someone planted next to the headstone shines like a pearl necklace encircling the delicate neck of a dead lover. Was Calvin the perpetrator of this fire? Did he carry his gun with him? I imagine him holding Renée's arm in a vise-like grip with his gun aimed at her mother's skull. "You two have spurned the man who supported you, defiled your father, *lied* about me. Now we'll burn together." The carnage of the Douglas family, who shone briefly like morning stars in Paris, only to fade away.

What did his eyes hide when his mouth was speaking to Renée? Did she answer, or look away at her mother's eyes? "You can't burn the dead," she'd say. "There's something inviolable about them, ringed round hard like frozen marbles to finger when the night stretches out too endlessly." Yes—that grave alone, among all the others, is still fresh and cold and welcoming to the delicate birds among the burning flowers. And now...where are they?

Indifference is a kind of power. Because I've decided to simply observe my pursuit of Renée. Something in me has been revitalized as if a crucible of sun-filled water buoyed my body, saying, "All is well now, Elizabeth." And my own mother's face appears to me, beautiful and benign. All the rancorous competition and despair of my childhood slowly disappears. I could say to her, "My brother walks among us, Mother, reborn years ago. His spirit is always with me now. Completely gentle, he was, with little dogs and rabbits. He was playful with all living things and completely honest in all his perceptions, especially in the amazingly splendid photographs of his friends."

Coming out of the graveyard, I take the path to the left. A pondering sunset hangs over the darkening trees. I walk another half mile up a terraced hill, and there, pushed under an overarching oak, sits Calvin's Citroën.

25

As I approach the house, I hear Renée saying, "This is the last time you'll humiliate me before all the world."

I sit beneath the graceful dormer window with my head bowed into my arms. Renée's voice sounds deeply grief-stricken as she berates Calvin.

"I was only twelve! Why didn't you shield me, educate me? You had money, books. Instead you performed the worst atrocity anyone can—you raped your own daughter! I should report you for arson, but I can't allow any more humiliation!"

I'm aroused from her voice by the stinging noise of a hard slap. I feel my own face flinch with pain. I remember a tremble in my hips. I take a couple of flying steps up the abrupt stone porch, push at the heavy door. I look up—Renée! Finally I see *her!* She's smaller than I thought she'd be, thin and very dark, with black hair cut blunt like a boy's. She's pointing a .45 at Calvin. Her right hand is shaking uncontrollably. He's sitting at her feet, eyes dilated, frightened. For a minute I think she's going to turn it on me—and then I see the terror in her eyes, the sobs just beneath her breasts.

"Elizabeth!" Calvin struggles up from his childish position of pleading. "Elizabeth, you've come to *my* home in Fuveau. Welcome, my dear!"

Renée's face is ecstatically relieved, as if she, more than I, were waiting for someone.

"Are you actually Elizabeth? Has he harmed you? I thought he brought you here."

"I'm okay now." I blink back tears of happiness. Her lovely thin face looks so weary.

"I called Mia three weeks ago. There were reports Calvin had captured an American woman. I feared the worst!"

"Renée, stop that this moment! I gave that child over ten thousand francs and kept her clean and safe."

Renée faces him with her gun. He crouches again on the floor.

"You gave me *no* money!" I exclaim. "You know that's not true. I'm trying to find a way out of this nightmare."

Calvin stands, then totters.

"It's never too late, Elizabeth, my dear. Let me extend an invitation to you now!"

"An invitation?"

"To break out of your rut, my sweet, and accept my generosity."

"It's not me who's in a rut!"

Renée tries to push Calvin into his chair, but he's begun to wave his arms.

"Renée, she needed a respite, so I wrote and invited her. Don't you think she's pretty?"

"Invited me where?"

"Here, my delicate one. Don't you remember our house exchange?"

"You! The lawyer from Fuveau whose letter gave me a way out! It was your house!"

"This very one, little Elizabeth!" He suddenly collapses into the chair.

Calvin's demented eyes—still staring at me from the newsprint—the article I'll never forget. Those desperate eyes...guiding me, telling me, like his eyes foresaw this scene—maybe—so many years ago. As if he knew I'd be here today, this September, 1968, repeating something...for me? For him? Were the conversations with Cecilia like that? Always some outrageous déjà vu? As if she and I had histories so old one couldn't talk about them, as if they couldn't belong to any one century. Where is Cecilia today?

I look around, walk to the mirror. The body in the mirror forces me to face it. I see myself suddenly older, thinner, my angry body fighting back. When I was with Cecilia I was so full of loathing and confusion about my volitionless body, hoping against all odds to get away from my sighing unhappiness. And saying yes to him, I looked not for a deliverer, since I no longer imagined there could be such a thing, but a place with sun and flowers, to soothe me, help me feel my strength again. He was even appealing then...said he worked continuously...commuted to Aix so he didn't know his own neighbors well enough to send me their phone numbers...a measure of something...my unawareness, I guess.

The chair he's sitting in should have been my dreaming chair. Instead, because of some twists in fate, because I was kidnapped by a charlatan, because the political upheavals in Paris called to me, I went and awakened.

"How did you find my Berkeley address, you old fool?"

"Make her leave me alone, Renée. I'm a *good* man, feet solidly planted in the ground, hands reaching out...I just missed you, Renée."

"Where'd you find me? I'm getting impatient."

"Darling, darling Elizabeth. I did not neglect the proper channels of international exchange. I answered your ad in *Le Figaro,* and I was very thorough. I saw your lovely photograph on the back of your book, the dark hair, so like Renée."

"So you're Michel Giraudoux? The one who wanted to take some refresher courses in the Legal Studies Program at Berkeley?"

"The name sounded feasible, my dear. My own great-grandfather was a very famous lawyer."

"Where's my book?"

He tries to stand but can't.

"Renée, go to my suitcase. On the top, next to your photograph, give her that prissy little book...."

He sticks out his index finger, makes his right hand into a gun, and points it at my face.

Renée holds up the rewrite of my dissertation on Djuna Barnes. I want to mangle it. Another woman writer who couldn't survive, who couldn't manage her money. Renée fixes her eyes on me, and for a moment I can see she resembles Calvin.

"You could have been my twin," she says.

"Yes!" I can hardly answer her.

"Renée, darling, I beg you! Clear me of this."

Renée puts the gun on the table beside her, never releasing her hand from it.

"Elizabeth, did he hurt you?"

"Not physically. But he wanted me psychologically sick, so I wouldn't leave him."

"You too, huh? When I was fifteen he had the gall to drag me to a psychiatrist, with some trumped-up charge of hysteria."

"Am I to be killed by your ungratefulness, too? Your mother would never allow this rebellion, Renée. She was a *real* lady!" Calvin begins to weep and shake his fist at her. Renée turns to me.

"We've got to sedate him. Then we'll figure out what to do."

"Did the *gendarmes* see him? He started the fire, didn't he?"

"Yes, like a lunatic he tried to burn Mother's grave. But it didn't work! I don't know whether the *gendarmes* saw him or not. I pushed him out of the cemetery the minute the fire began. He was clutching his gun, threatening suicide and murder. I knocked it from his hand, told him he was too impotent to commit suicide. I marched him home with the gun held to the small of his back. If anyone saw us, they would have seen a tender daughter assisting her crippled old father!"

Renée understands. She wants to kill him too. But unexpectedly I see her face redden, as if the full humiliation of endless compromise has spread across her eyes.

"I'm ashamed we had to meet like this," she says.

"Oh, Renée, you've just been through a terrible experience. Let me help you. I can, you know."

"What will we do with him?"

"Is there Valium here?"

"Yes, his houses are like pharmacies. They're not places for people."

"Get it, then," I say and, turning, continue, "Calvin, we're going to give you a pill for your sleep. You'll finally be able to sleep." His face sags in all its dry lines of humorlessness. He sighs as if relieved to be free of his will, as if he wants to die in a deep sleep of forgetfulness.

26

His snoring reminds me of those terrible months in Paris, the suffocating blue satin bedsheets and the recurring nightmares. Renée's resting, exhausted and dreaming in Calvin's large leather recliner.

I want to stare at Calvin now, to read the lines in his face when it's safe, when his hands are asleep. There's an alarming whiteness to his bedroom. Really, as Renée said, Calvin's houses are not for the living.

His mouth turns down in an exaggerated horseshoe. Next to his bed, an empty bottle of Valium has been turned on its side. Surely Renée knew how much to give him. But he's so awfully quiet. I walk over to the pearl washbasin and wash my fingers. He groans when he hears the waters splattering. He shifts his legs. When I return, his right arm rests outside the blankets. The pulsating soft skin of his forearm beats like the gill of a beached fish. It's strange to think so weak and fragile a creature could also be brutal. I don't know what I expected to learn. Only a kindly pathos remains for me, as if his body were already emptied of its organs.

Renée stirs. She glances at the chaise lounge again, as if she's only now believing that the furniture will stay fixed in some real alignment of wood to stone, and stone to the limestone earth beneath us. Her eyes are emerald green like the eyes of a fierce tigress keeping her young from harm.

"It's been fifteen years since I was here. Mother's house looks something like it did before. I still see her sense of humor on the walls. That Paul Klee print above the green chaise lounge—you like his—?"

"Oh—it's charming! Were you here on vacations—with your parents?"

"For a time, when the house was my mother's, it was like a vacation with her. Then Calvin captured it for his "private practice," as he called it. All the walls were painted white. A nurse padded about in white buck shoes."

"How'd your mother get hold of such a fabulous house?"

"Mother was French, you see, French Provençal to be exact. This was her family's home. Calvin married her in America...when she studied at Johns Hopkins. He graduated from Johns Hopkins. She became his wife though *she* should have been the internist. The situation which ruined most women merely troubled my mother, it didn't ruin her. But France itself won out. Mother couldn't abide the snobbish Bostonians and their awful winters. 'Either you come with me to Paris or I go alone,' she said. Calvin was clever enough to get a postdoctoral post at the Pasteur Institute. Being the egotist he is, he planned to take her back to Boston. But she was too stubborn and fiery. So painting became her avocation in Paris. She learned it from Sonia Delaunay, who was our neighbor when I was born. Sonia Delaunay sometimes watched me when mother was working. Mother had five one-woman shows at different galleries on the West Bank."

"Do you think of yourself as French or American?"

"Neither."

"Why?"

"I can't remember Boston. The last time I saw my grandparents I was six. And the French—well, *God* might speak French, but Jesus wouldn't. He couldn't stand any language so absent from the sublime—or the naïve, for that matter."

"How do you identify yourself then?"

"I'm my *mother's* girl. I'm like her family. My aunt still lives nearby in Arles, "Aunt Vivien," she calls herself, and she's a superior horsewoman. *Those* two are my ancestors!"

I want to tell her about *my* view of Arles from the train and *my* months in the guest bedroom, with only Van Gogh's *Starry Night*, that painting Calvin gave me to console myself.

"Calvin bought me a racing bike when I was fourteen. He said we'd go into training together for the Tour de France. That's when it first happened."

"What?"

"He'd go away with me—for two or three days— 'pacing ourselves in the Loire Valley,' he'd tell Mother. She was too trusting, and I was too frightened to talk. At night when the other cyclists were camping in their sleeping bags, Calvin and I went to little inns. He'd order the innkeeper. 'Give me the biggest room you've got with two big beds! This daughter of mine's in training.' Then, at night he'd listen to me breathe and touch himself under the covers. Sometimes, beforehand, he'd walk over to me and pull down his pajamas, while I pretended to sleep. The mornings were hellish. He acted as if nothing had happened. He'd buy me a larger-than-usual breakfast with ham and heavy French bread and say casually, 'If your mother knew the vigor of our training, she'd be awfully upset. Her heart might fail. Mother mustn't know—for her *own* sake.'"

"Oh, god, Renée—I'm sorry. *Did* you ever confide in your mother?"

"She really *did* have a heart condition, so I didn't. But the fear never left me."

"Was there *anyone* to tell?"

"I began to have nightmares. In one recurring one, I tried to climb a mountain of coal...you must be bored with this accounting." Renée's face turns a greyish-white, and she looks down. I'm afraid she'll faint, so I help her to a chair.

"I'm not! I'm also getting over a severe shock, a woman who didn't respect me..."

"Who?"

"It's hard to talk about it. She was my therapist. She'd say, 'Elizabeth, your fantasies are so powerful—I can't resist them! Doesn't everyone tell you that?' And I loved her."

"It sounds like she betrayed you." Renée looks straight at me. Her eyes are wide open. "Very soon after the bicycle training that summer, Calvin took me to a psychiatrist, a friend of his. He told the man I was hysterical. I'd begun to write Mother letters I never sent, complaining of leg cramps. One day, my right leg hurt so badly I couldn't walk. The joints felt like they were on fire. Calvin fell into a fury! 'Get out of that god-damned bed and get yourself prepared for the *lycée* and your training, Renée. Will your mother and I never hear the end of it?' It was during that fall that Germaine, my special friend, visited me in the evenings. Germaine was beautiful and kind. She'd actually won fourth place in the Tour de France for younger contestants. She looked like Jeanne Moreau. I told her I never wanted to race again. I'd never let myself think of girls before. I never allowed myself feelings of love at all. But she went to bat for me. She told my coach I could never bicycle again. At night, on the weekends anyway, she'd massage my legs. After a while, she'd occasionally stay over with me. One thing followed another. I wanted to marry her. When Calvin realized that we cared for each other, he called her mother—I can't remember what he said. Except it was then he took me to Dr. Ebert."

"Did you ever see Germaine again?"

"Not for two years. The psychiatrist said I must never be tempted again, that it would end with me taking my life. He promised me lessons on the basic psychological concepts in addition to the sessions."

"Did you tell him about Calvin?"

"How could I? I just became more and more depressed. The day came when he talked about shock therapy. 'We'll have a limited series of shocks,' he promised. That night I packed and went to Arles to live with my Aunt Vivien. She kept me. She wrote Mother telling her about Calvin, and Mother never recovered from it."

Renée is my sister. She wears white starched blouses and boy's leather shoes. She transforms things. I can't disappoint her. I won't.

"Where is Germaine now?"

"You're not listening to what's important to me! Didn't you hear? Mother got sicker—her heart got weaker—she sent money, but she didn't want me to come home, ever. She couldn't stand between Calvin and me. I felt God was punishing me for being with Calvin and with Germaine."

"You seem so strong though—didn't you—"

"I was too young to understand it. My aunt bought a horse for me so we could ride together. But I couldn't go back to school. Not for many years."

Renée gets up to make tea.

"School was all I had," I said. "My teachers were everything—they had to be mother and father. I still need that kind of love." Only Renée can be trusted with my confession.

Renée hides her eyes, though I've already seen their sorrows. She holds my hand for only a moment.

"When we're in Paris, we'll walk in the Bois de Boulogne. We'll get out a lot. You do any sports?" she asks.

"Yeah, I swim and ride. I was jumping thoroughbreds when I left Berkeley!"

"Maybe we'll ride together then. What else do you do in Berkeley?"

"Oh, I teach, write the occasional article."

"Are your students high school students?"

"No, university…University of California students." This telling parts of my life to Renée doesn't seem implausible. For the first time in many months I remember what a good teacher I am. I feel happy and alive for the first time in years. "I don't ever want to see Cecilia again," I say. Something in me relaxes, lets in Renée's orderliness—her white shirts and comfortable jeans. A friend, an *honest* friend.

"Good! You must close the door on her."

"Renée, did anything happen here—with Calvin—in this house?"

"I can't tell you about that. Calvin's the same as dead to me." She has tears in her eyes. Turns to pour out the tea when there's a singularly surprising sound outside the front door.

"Who's there?" I walk to the door. "Julien! Come in!"

Julien looks frightened. "Where's Calvin? Are you safe, Elizabeth?"

"It's all over…and yes, I've never been so safe!"

Part Eight

Ascending

27

1 September, morning

I don't fear being alone or being spurned by another. I can leave whatever I have to leave. I know that now.

2 September

After people have left me alone a long time, I'm stronger, stretching out my longings to the evening star.

3 September

Colette has written me a letter to explain her long silence. "I don't regret anything we did," she boasts. "But I'm no longer sure I'm a lesbian. Jacques needs my sensitivity in such a cruel world as ours. Truth is, he thinks I'm a damned good artist! You know how doctors are, kidnapping culture wherever they find it. I guess I'll stay with him 'til I'm on my feet. You never grew up poor, like me. I don't expect you to understand. If I were a lesbian, you'd be it, my darling. For now, I send kisses." Over her signature, she's drawn a valentine-shaped face with one eye winking.

4 September

Renée's possessed by the necessity of emptying herself. She doesn't do it in fiction. She writes news analyses which she composes trepidatiously: "The psychedelic '60s are about opening ourselves to sensations and messages from above and below. The mystical vibrations between planets and people are what the French students understood. They didn't fail—we did."

5 September

Mother's finally found my address. Her letter came today, with a check. "Please forgive me, Elizabeth. I was so bereaved with grief, I hardly even realized I was accusing you. When will I ever see you again?"

So I call Mother, tell her I've thrown two pennies at the feet of Aphrodite in a weird little courtyard in the Marais. I tell her that we have a lot to say to one another now.

7 September

Last night I heard the cat's paw fall in Calvin's garden. Though he's far away in Boston now with some distant cousins, I still hear his voice. Renée's cleaning the study to make it more comfortable.

8 September, afternoon

"I feel like a performing seal." That's what Colette sings as she pirouettes through *her* gallery space at the City Museum of Paris. She's joined the ranks of the modern, so she imagines. She arranges long tubes on the walls, made from photographic fragments: the nipple of a breast, the knuckles on an arthritic hand, semen dripping from a penis—"ugly stuff to shock the bourgeoisie," she says. Knowing nothing about nineteenth-century art or ideas, she picks the brains of whoever's available for this chic phrase or that. "Meet me at La Palette near the rue de Seine tomorrow," she says. "I want to begin my friendship with you." I laugh, wondering always at my past infatuations.

20 September

When you go to Versailles, you either get the train from Montparnasse or the R.E.R. from Austerlitz.

24 September

Djuna Barnes never compromised. She wrote Natalie Barney: "I've refused the publishers my right to 'Nights Among the Horses.' I won't let a past story of mine be anthologized with these shallow opportunists." I'm still searching for that balance between rebellion and reason in my own life. Odd that Calvin first saw my picture on the back of my biography of Barnes. I wrote about her then without discerning her habitually desperate courage. Now Calvin has tested mine.

26 September, morning

Last night I had the strangest dreams. I can't yet analyze them. I was walking in St.-Chapelle and looked down at my stomach and realized I was pregnant. Then I thought, No—it's Jessica who's pregnant. Then Jessica was walking beside me. But the focus was still on my stomach. It's not big enough for a baby, I thought! And then the dream changed—I felt the birth pains and a baby girl with black curled hair and long fingernails spoke to me as if she were ten.

27 September

I want to describe myself like a painting I've studied closely for a very long time, like the face of my daughter, like a strong ship that takes me safely through the wildest storm.

28 September

There's no actual judicial retribution for most of the May rioters. Just their silencing. No reforms in university education. And the same old standoff between labor and the bosses. When Colette and I return to the École des Beaux Arts, no red flags hang from the towers. Silk-screening and coffee-making are merely memories now.

"What's become of your fight against the competitive examinations?" I ask. No one answers me.

"The bourgeois assholes are buying our posters," a woman student says. "The flaming posters from the Atelier Populaire of the École des Beaux Arts are hanging on the walls of policemen and shopkeepers!" She sneers.

"Every view of things which is not strange is false."

"Mankind will not live free until the last capitalist has been hanged with the entrails of the last bureaucrat."

In my mind, I'm back in the streets, hiding behind the fiery automobiles and pyramids of rubbish. I want to say, "I'll never forget you," but for some reason I don't.

1 October

Renée and I have become like sisters. One night she cooks, then I cook. I've started a novel, I tell her. "What about?" she asks. "It's still emerging," I say. She doesn't press me. I read what I wrote last night, words like "hunger," "thunder," "passion." I write now in an explosive state, in an atmosphere of settling accounts where invectives take the place of slaps in the face. I feel a faint trembling, as if the insults I've swallowed so long without responding are about to erupt from my chest, splitting it into millions of fragments of grief and anger. But I want also to write about magic and forgiveness, the magic some feel only on LSD, Allen Ginsberg's *Howl*. The violent disdain, the cruel humor, the sorceries of American scenery with its frizzy-haired hippies on the hideous highways and the fire-breathing preachers in the American South, the children with their red-red hula hoops, and the testy feminists fighting for their rights.

10 October

The surface of the Gulf lay rippling and warm,
We'd lower the string, and they'd hold on.
The wood would be warm,
And the crabs, fat and coral-colored, would clench the string
All the way up.

12 October

I see a rim of bamboo trees surrounding a clearing in that house we had in Back Bay, my brother. That Mississippi bamboo grove with all its ants and burr stickers. Father heard us then, all whispers and songs. He heard the rehearsal of our poems as he hacked away at the smooth-stemmed bamboo in his hot hideaway. I wish my brother were here to meet Julien—and Renée.

13 October

Listening to Mozart's *Requiem*—death's ecstasy and my complicity with Mozart every bit as real as my complicitous anger with Cecilia. America/France—France/America. In one nation, the revolution ruled with rock music to shock the American soul out of its numb sleep, but in the other, in France, the revolution was like fire and ice, both a searing violence and volatility, an ironically serious debate.

14 October

At Berkeley, I knew some boys who blew their brains out on LSD. No one could figure them out. I began to notice small things—their sentences without verbs, and their slouching backs.

15 October

The sun appeared a furious white today. Walking near the quays next to the Seine, I thought I saw Calvin, his head straining forward—as if his bloody nostrils were leading him closer to the place where his enemies hide.

16 October

Renée says Calvin is dying—his liver gets weaker and weaker every day.

18 October

Renée believes no one ever *sees* a lesbian on the Paris streets.

"Just because we're invisible now doesn't mean we'll always be," I reply.

"But when?" she asks. Soon we'll be seen, respected; we'll be known. And the lights will explode from the sands of sunshine—the vacationing souls all tanned in bright self-recognition will dance all over the land.

21 October

Julien says because of me he now really loves women—no longer theorizes about their political applicability...

24 October

Last night I believed I was an abandoned lover whom no one loved. I heard the thud of hooves on the black boulevard outside my window.

30 October

My daughters are my shining lights, Renée. They've always been that way for me. And I promise you, I raised them. I had to make it up day by day with no scripts and no real partners. Now they run like the young deer I've watched in forests, with their exuberance and anticipation.

Jessica wrote to say she's dancing in a spring concert at school. Will I be home soon? She wants to know.

31 October

I believe I *will* be home soon, Jessica. For I don't care how often Persephone goes to the underworld—I always hear her horses of determination, thundering out of their heavy opaque graves just in time to see the apple trees flinging down their intricate pink flowers on spring lawns all over the world.

Photo by PhotoWorks

Madeline Moore is an Associate Professor of English Literature at UC Santa Cruz and the author of *The Short Season Between Two Silences: The Mystical and the Political in the Novels of Virginia Woolf* as well as numerous articles, essays, and poems.

Other Titles Available From Spinsters Ink

All The Muscle You Need, Diana McRae	$8.95
As You Desire, Madeline Moore	$9.95
Being Someone, Ann MacLeod	$9.95
Cancer in Two Voices, Butler & Rosenblum	$12.95
Child of Her People, Anne Cameron	$8.95
Considering Parenthood, Cheri Pies	$12.95
Desert Years, Cynthia Rich	$7.95
Elise, Claire Kensington	$7.95
Final Rest, Mary Morell	$9.95
Final Session, Mary Morell	$9.95
High and Outside, Linnea A. Due	$8.95
The Journey, Anne Cameron	$9.95
The Lesbian Erotic Dance, JoAnn Loulan	$12.95
Lesbian Passion, JoAnn Loulan	$12.95
Lesbian Sex, JoAnn Loulan	$12.95
Lesbians at Midlife, ed. by Sang, Warshow & Smith	$12.95
Life Savings, Linnea Due	$10.95
Look Me in the Eye, 2nd Ed., Macdonald & Rich	$8.95
Love and Memory, Amy Oleson	$9.95
Modern Daughters and the Outlaw West, Melissa Kwasny	$9.95
The Solitary Twist, Elizabeth Pincus	$9.95
Thirteen Steps, Bonita L. Swan	$8.95
The Two-Bit Tango, Elizabeth Pincus	$9.95
Vital Ties, Karen Kringle	$10.95
Why Can't Sharon Kowalski Come Home? Thompson & Andrzejewski	$10.95

Spinsters titles are available at your local booksellers, or by mail order through Spinsters Ink. A free catalogue is available upon request.

Please include $1.50 for the first title ordered, and 50 cents for every title thereafter. Visa and Mastercard accepted.

Spinsters Ink was founded in 1978 to produce vital books for diverse women's communities. In 1986 we merged with Aunt Lute Books to become Spinsters/Aunt Lute. In 1990, the Aunt Lute Foundation became an independent non-profit publishing program. In 1992, Spinsters moved to Minneapolis.

Spinsters Ink is committed to publishing full-length novels and non-fiction works that deal with significant issues in women's lives from a feminist perspective: books that not only name crucial issues in women's lives, but more importantly encourage change and growth; books that help make the best in our lives more possible. We are particularly interested in creative works by lesbians.

spinsters ink
p.o. box 300170
minneapolis, mn 55403